Justin wasn't planning on moving to Gillham. He doesn't have a reason, except that his best friend has just bonded with his mate and now lives there. But when Justin helps Pryderi move, he meets Pryderi's brother, Yedley — his mate.

Yedley has no idea what he's doing. He has a chance at a new life, but he doesn't know where to start until Fate takes that decision away from him and puts Justin in his path. But meeting his mate doesn't solve Yedley's problems. Justin is there for him, but Yedley still needs to come out to his parents and find his way in life. He needs to let Justin become close, even though he's still trying to get over his kidnapping and the time he spent with the Beasts, and he doesn't know how to do that.

The danger the Beasts represent is still looming, and Justin is glad when his transfer request to Gillham is accepted, because it means he can be close to his mate and keep him safe. It's a new start for both him and Yedley, but they'll have to find their way around each other — and around their bond.

Justin
Copyright © 2019 Catherine Lievens
ISBN: 978-1-4874-2709-2
Cover art by Angela Waters

Published by eXtasy Books Inc or
Devine Destinies, an imprint of eXtasy Books Inc

Look for us online at:
www.eXtasybooks.com or www.devinedestinies.com

Justin
Council Enforcers Book 21

By

Catherine Lievens

CHAPTER ONE

Yedley was happy. He hated that it had taken him being kidnapped to find his brother, but it was better than not having Pryderi at all. He could do without having to help his brother move, though.

"I thought you were going to help me?" Pryderi asked when Yedley opened the door of Calvin's room.

Yedley grinned at him. "I'll help you unpack." There was no way he was walking up and down the stairs, not when he knew Calvin was uncomfortable with having someone who wasn't part of their small family in the apartment. Pryderi had asked his best friend to help him move, and while Yedley didn't blame him since it meant he didn't have to help, he wished something could be done to make Calvin more comfortable.

"I suppose it's better than nothing. Lunch is ready."

"We'll be right there."

Pryderi walked away, and Yedley closed the door and turned toward Calvin. Calvin was on his bed, curled up with his back against the wall. It was his usual position, as if he expected someone to attack him. He probably did, considering what had happened to him. "You heard Pryderi. Lunch is ready."

Calvin looked like he might decide not to have lunch, but he'd already tried that a few times and Yedley hadn't gone along with it. Calvin needed to eat after all the time he'd spent between labs and the Beasts, and Yedley wouldn't allow him to stay in his room only because Pryderi's friend was there.

"He's my brother's best friend," Yedley said. "Pryderi wouldn't have asked him to help if he didn't trust him."

Calvin sighed. "I'm not trying to make this difficult, I swear."

"I know you're not. Come on. You can peek inside the kitchen and decide if you want to eat with us or bring your lunch back here."

Yedley hated the thought of Calvin eating alone in his bedroom, but he didn't want Calvin to freak out because a stranger was there. It would take him some time to get used to having people who weren't planning to hurt him around. Yedley didn't want to push him too hard.

Pryderi was leaving the bathroom when Yedley and Calvin got there. Pryderi waited for them to wash their hands, keeping his distance from Calvin. Yedley was grateful his brother did that without having to be asked. The three of them—Yedley, Pryderi, and Nate—might not know what Calvin had been through, but they were aware it had been hell for him, and they all wanted him to be happy sharing the apartment with them as a family. There was a lot of walking around on eggshells and making sure he wasn't freaking out, but it was a small price to pay.

"Are you sure your brother's friend is okay?" Calvin asked, leaning close to Yedley as they walked toward the kitchen.

"Well, I've never met him, but I trust my brother, and if he trusts this guy, then I do, too."

The corner of Calvin's lips curled up. "That's a lot of trust."

And that was precisely what Calvin was missing in his life, but Yedley didn't say that. Calvin was aware of it, and there was no need to hurt him more than he already was.

Yedley followed Calvin into the kitchen, but he froze as soon as he saw the man already in there. *Justin.* It couldn't be anyone else, since there was only one person helping today.

Justin was Yedley's mate.

What was Yedley supposed to do? He wanted to talk to Justin. He wanted to run away.

He'd never imagined he'd meet his mate. He probably should have, but he'd been so busy and worried over his kidnapping and the time he'd spent with the Beasts, and of course, possibly having to come out to his parents if he ever got free, that the thought hadn't gone through his mind.

And now he was staring at his mate. As far as he could see, Justin hadn't realized something was happening. That was good. No matter how much Yedley wanted to talk to Justin, he had no idea what he'd say to him, or even if he'd be able to get a word out of his mouth. "He's single," Pryderi murmured. He tried to push Yedley into the room, but Yedley wasn't moving. He *couldn't* move.

He forced himself to swallow. "You're sure?" He was confused, but knowing that his mate didn't have a boyfriend made him feel better.

"Yeah. He's one of my best friends. I'd know if he had someone, even though I haven't been spending a lot of time in Whitedell lately."

Yedley nodded, mostly to himself. He was relieved he wouldn't have to take his mate away from someone else, but that didn't mean he had even the slightest idea of what to do now. "Good."

"Yeah?"

God. What would Pryderi think about this? Would he be happy that his brother and his best friend were mates? Or would he get angry? Yedley supposed there was only one way to find out. "Yeah. I'd hate to think of my mate with another man." Or woman. Yedley didn't know Justin. He didn't even know if Justin was gay, or if he liked men at all.

"What?" Pryderi looked nonplussed as if he didn't quite believe what Yedley had just told him.

Yedley didn't blame him. "He's my mate." Yedley didn't

want to analyze his feelings about it too closely. They were a jumble of hope that Justin would want him in his life and they could be happy, fear that Justin *wouldn't* want him, happiness at having found his mate, and a whole bunch of other things Yedley hadn't even been aware he could feel at the same time.

Pryderi blinked. "Justin?"

Yedley understood being shocked by the news better than anyone, but was Pryderi serious? "Who do you think? Calvin? I would have told you already if that were the case." And since the only other man in the room was Nate and he couldn't be Yedley's mate since he was Pryderi's, it shouldn't take long for Pryderi to realize Yedley wasn't lying.

Pryderi looked from Yedley to Justin, then back at Yedley again. "I didn't expect this."

"I didn't either, trust me. I have no clue what to do with a mate. I don't even know what to do with my *life*."

Pryderi grimaced. "He won't push for anything. I know Justin. He's a good guy."

"I hope you're right."

"I've known him for years. If there's one thing I'm sure of, it's that he's a good guy."

Yedley nodded. He wasn't sure what else to say. He knew the others in the room expected him and Pryderi to sit at the table and have lunch, but he didn't think he could do that. How was he supposed to face Justin and not blurt out that they were mates? Besides, Yedley was pretty sure Justin was a shifter, and that meant that once he got close enough, he'd realize Yedley was his mate.

"I know you're not ready for this," Pryderi said. "It's understandable. You don't *have* to be ready for it."

Yedley wrinkled his nose. "He's going to find out if I sit at the table with you and the others."

"It's not a bad thing. Or were you planning on keeping it a secret from him?"

Yedley shook his head. "I have no idea."

Pryderi looked around the room again. "You should probably talk to Justin alone. I doubt either of you wants to be this exposed for this conversation."

Yedley certainly didn't want to. He wanted to go back to his room and hide away, but also to crawl into Justin's lap and ask his mate to keep him safe.

Pryderi cleared his throat. "Why don't you go downstairs to the bar? It's closed right now, so you won't be disturbed. I'll tell Justin to follow you there, and you can tell him whatever you feel up to." He squeezed Yedley's arm. "Everything will be okay. I promise."

Yedley wanted to believe his brother, but he wasn't sure he could.

Justin hadn't missed the way Pryderi and his brother were hovering at the kitchen door. He wasn't sure what was happening, but he wasn't about to stick his nose into it. It wasn't his business, and both Nate's and Pryderi's brothers had been through enough that the last thing Justin wanted was to scare them even more.

He made sure to stay as far as possible away from Calvin, who was now sitting next to Nate. Calvin was so obviously nervous that Justin wanted to reassure him, but that would only make things worse.

"Thanks for helping," Nate said.

Justin shrugged. "Of course I helped. Pryderi is my best friend." And losing him was hard on Justin, even though he realized how dramatic he was being by thinking that.

He wasn't losing Pryderi. Even though Pryderi was moving to Gilham to be with his mate, they'd still see each other. They'd still be best friends.

But it would be weird not to work side by side with

Pryderi. It would be strange not to have him at his door in the morning telling him to move his ass or to turn to tell him something and not find him there. Justin was happy for Pryderi, of course, but he couldn't help being sad.

"When are you going back? You can stay for dinner if you want. I'm sure Pryderi would be happy if you did," Nate said.

Justin was tempted to say yes, but he supposed he needed to start living without his best friend by his side almost twenty-four seven.

"Justin?" Pryderi called out before Justin could answer.

Justin turned toward him. Pryderi's brother was gone, and that made Justin frown. Had he scared Yedley so much that the man couldn't have lunch with them? "Is something wrong?"

Pryderi rubbed the back of his neck. "Not wrong, exactly, but Yedley wants to talk to you."

"He does?" Justin had no idea why, since he'd never met the man before. And even today, he'd made sure to stay as far away from Yedley as possible, wanting to give the man his space.

"He went downstairs to the bar."

Justin frowned. "Did he?"

"He'll tell you what's happening."

Justin knew Pryderi wouldn't be telling him this if it weren't important, so he got up. He was hungry, but that could wait. "He's downstairs?"

"That's what he said, yes." Pryderi hesitated. "Keep an open mind. Okay?"

Justin had no idea why Pryderi thought of telling him that was important, but he nodded. He walked past his best friend, patting his shoulder on his way out of the kitchen. He might not have been expecting this, but that didn't mean he was angry. Confused, yes. But not angry.

The bar was weird without any customers—too silent and

smelling of detergent. It took Justin a second to find Yedley, who was wedged between the wall and the counter.

"Yedley?" Justin said, trying not to get so close he'd scare Yedley.

Yedley jumped a little, and Justin took a step back. Maybe he'd been too close. "Justin."

"Pryderi told me you needed to talk to me?"

"I do."

"I'm listening." He still had no idea what Yedley needed to talk to him about. He might be aware of what Yedley had been through, but this was the first time they'd met. Pryderi had wanted to introduce them, but both Yedley and Calvin had spent the day in Calvin's bedroom, and Pryderi hadn't pushed. Justin hadn't been offended, not with what he knew about their history.

To Justin's surprise, Yedley hopped off the stool. He moved hesitantly, but he was getting closer to Justin, and Justin didn't know what to do. He decided that staying still was probably the best thing, for Yedley's sake.

Yedley stopped only inches away from Justin. He was so close that Justin could see the brown flecks in his green eyes. So close that Justin could smell him.

So close that Justin realized why Yedley had wanted to talk to him alone.

He forced himself not to move. He was in shock, but he didn't want to scare Yedley away. It had to have taken him a lot of courage to come so close to Justin. He could have stayed where he was and told him the truth, told him they were mates, but instead, he was letting Justin realize it on his own.

Justin didn't think it mattered, but he was grateful he'd been able to recognize his mate's scent rather than having Yedley tell him about their connection. It made something inside him settle and his werewolf purr, which wasn't something that happened often.

"This is where you say something," Yedley said.

Justin chuckled. "I want to."

"But you're in shock and confused. Trust me, I know how that feels."

Of course he did. That was why he'd frozen when he'd walked into the kitchen earlier. He was a Nix, and that meant he'd realized Justin was his mate the first time he saw him. That would have been a shock for anyone, and Justin didn't know how to help. "Let's just say I didn't expect this when I agreed to help Pryderi move."

Yedley snorted and stepped away. He looked more relaxed, and that made Justin feel better. "I didn't expect this, either." He raked a hand through his hair. "I mean, I haven't even come out to my parents yet. The only person who knows I'm gay is my brother."

Justin's stomach turned heavy, but he wouldn't assume. He couldn't, not when he barely knew his mate. "I know part of your history," he started.

"You mean the part where I was kidnapped and was supposed to end up in a lab but was instead dumped in the middle of the street by a Beast."

"That part, yes. But Pryderi also told me about *his* past, and I understand why you haven't talked to your parents yet."

Yedley rubbed his face. "I don't how I feel about you being my brother's best friend."

"I'm sorry." Justin hoped Yedley wasn't about to ask him to choose, because he wasn't sure he could do that.

"That's not what I meant. I don't care that you're Pryderi's best friend, not beyond the fact that it means you're aware of our past. You know how I behaved and that I didn't support him the way I should have when he came out to our parents. I wish you didn't. I'm not proud of my past, and I know it probably looks like I'm a hypocrite, since I'm gay, too."

That made more sense, and it was a relief. "Like you said,

it's your *past*. It's been a while since it happened, and it's obvious you've been through a lot. I won't hold that against you. But we should probably talk things out."

Yedley turned away as if he couldn't look Justin in the eye when he talked. "I don't think there's much to talk about. I knew I was gay when my brother came out. I should have supported him and stood up to our parents. Instead, I watched as they insulted him and told him he wasn't welcome in our home anymore. They told him he was a freak, a monster. They tried to get him to marry a woman because they thought it would fix him. And there I was, the same as him, but too much of a coward to do anything about it. I let him leave without even trying to stop him or to stay in contact with him."

"He doesn't hold that against you." Pryderi never had. He and Justin had talked about this more than once, and Justin hadn't understood. He wasn't sure he did now, but he wanted to. He wouldn't hold the past against Yedley.

"Maybe he should. You know what he did. Even though we hadn't seen each other since then, when he found out what I'd been through, he welcomed me into his home. I don't deserve him, or what he's doing for me. I don't know how to thank him. And I don't know how you could look beyond what I did and give me a chance."

Yedley expected Justin to tell him he couldn't. He didn't know how Pryderi had managed to look past what he'd done and forgive him, but they were brothers. That had to have played a role in it. Justin, on the other hand, didn't know Yedley. They might be mates, but it didn't mean he would forgive him or that they had to be together.

"Do you really think I'd give up the possibility of having you in my life because of what happened years ago?" Justin asked. "Wait. Of course you do. We don't know each other. But you're wrong."

Yedley forced himself to face his mate. "I am?"

"Like I told you before, it's in the past. You did the wrong thing, and you're aware of that. I understand why you feel guilty, but I'm not sure you should. You put a lot of the blame on your shoulders when really, you should put it on your parents. You didn't want to lose them. No one wants to lose their parents, especially not for something they have no control over."

"But Pryderi didn't hesitate. He told them."

Justin snorted. "You think he didn't hesitate? He did, trust me. We talked about it, and he told me how hard deciding to tell them was. He knew how they'd react. He hoped they wouldn't kick him out, but he had a plan in case they did."

"Which was to become an enforcer." It made sense, but it didn't help Yedley feel less guilty.

"Exactly. He was aware he'd lose his parents, and while it hurt, I think that losing you hurt him more. You two were close before that happened, weren't you?"

"We were." And Yedley hoped they'd become close again. He'd been in town for only a few weeks, and Pryderi had been focused on catching the guys who'd kidnapped him, but he thought things were going well.

"I'm not trying to say he didn't feel betrayed by your reaction, but it's not something you need to talk about with me. Have you and Pryderi talked things out?"

"Somewhat." Yedley had told his brother he was gay and that he wouldn't go back to their parents, but they probably needed to have a more in-depth conversation. Yedley wasn't over this yet, and he couldn't imagine Pryderi was.

"You should probably do that."

Yedley nodded and looked down. "But like I was saying, I'd understand if you didn't want anything to do with me. I know I wasn't the best person in the past, and that things are different now, but—"

"I'm going to stop you right there. I did things in the past I'm not proud of. I can't change them, and neither can you. The most important thing about this isn't what happened years ago but what happens now and what will happen in the future. You know you were wrong. You're trying to change things, to make sure the future is different from the past. You won't choose your parents over Pryderi again, will you?"

"Of course not. They were wrong when they kicked him out because he's gay. They shouldn't have, and I should have done more to stop them."

"But you weren't ready to lose them. They're your parents. It's understandable. They should love you and be there for you, and they haven't been. You had to choose between them and your brother, and at the time, you did what was best for you."

But it wasn't what was best for Yedley now. He hadn't been lying when he told his brother he was never going back. He didn't want to go back to the tribe. He didn't want to see his parents again. He'd thought they cared for him, but they hadn't cared enough to contact his enforcer brother when he'd been kidnapped. The man they considered their only son had disappeared, and because they hadn't wanted to talk to their gay son, they hadn't even contacted the enforcers. Pryderi could have helped. He could have found Yedley and maybe even Calvin, but instead, they'd had to rely on one of the Beasts to be freed.

Not caring enough to contact Pryderi was the last nail in the coffin. Yedley hadn't wanted to go back anyway, but now he was sure he wouldn't.

He wanted a new life, and he had a chance at it. He could have his brother, and now, a mate.

It was overwhelming. He didn't have any kind of

experience with men, and especially not with mates. His parents weren't mates, and while Pryderi and Nate were, Yedley hadn't had much time to observe them. It was obvious they loved each other, and that they were comfortable around each other, but it didn't help.

Was Yedley supposed to kiss Justin now? They were mates, and that meant that if things went well, they'd eventually bond. The thought was terrifying but also soothing in a way. Yedley would never have to be alone again.

After he'd lost his brother because being such a coward, Yedley had been alone. He'd still been living with his parents, but he'd avoided them as much as possible, and he'd planned to leave the tribe.

But he hadn't. It had been easier to stick around and continue living his everyday life. He'd avoided his parents and worked for the tribe. Before he knew it, years had passed, and he'd still been there.

Until he'd been kidnapped. Maybe he should be grateful to the Beasts for taking him. If they hadn't, he doubted he'd have left the tribe. He could too easily imagine that he might have eventually given in to his parents' requests to get married and have children. He might have wanted to find Pryderi, but leaving the life he knew and the people in it had felt impossible. It had been petrifying, and while Yedley wasn't proud of that, he couldn't deny it. It had been easier to continue behaving as if nothing had changed.

Then everything had.

Yedley knew he was lucky the Beasts hadn't transferred him to the lab like they'd intended to. He was lucky the man in charge had been arrested. He'd never been through what Calvin had been through, and he never would. He had no reason to complain or to have nightmares, and he needed to get over it. This was his chance at a new life, a life he wanted.

"I'm choosing my brother this time," he said.

Justin smiled. "Good. I don't think I've ever seen Pryderi this happy."

"That's probably because of Nate, not me."

Justin shrugged. "I think it's a mix. He's happy Nate finally gave in, of course, but I know he didn't ever expect to have you in his life again. This is a new start for both of you, and I'm glad you won't go home, especially knowing what I do about your parents."

"So where do we go from here?"

"Wherever you want."

"There are two of us in this relationship." Yedley paused. "Not that we have a relationship yet, of course. But you know what I mean."

To Yedley's relief, Justin wasn't running away — yet.

"I know what you meant, yes. And it's true we're both important in this situation, but we shouldn't ignore what you've been through. You were kidnapped, and you would have ended up in a lab if that man hadn't freed you."

"I didn't, though. Nothing happened to me."

"That's not true. Even though you weren't experimented on like some of the other people we found with you were, it doesn't mean nothing happened to you. Being kidnapped was no doubt terrifying, and, understandably, you need space. I won't push you into anything you aren't comfortable with."

"I don't know what I'm comfortable with. It's not about the kidnapping, or at least, not just that. I have no idea what I'm doing."

"You never came out to your parents. Does that mean you only had relationships with women?"

"It does." And it had been hard. His parents weren't going around asking the women he'd been with if they had sex, of course, but if he'd avoided sex entirely, that would have gotten around, and he hadn't wanted to be the center of tribe gossip. So yes, he'd had sex with a few women, even though he hadn't felt attracted to them. He was lucky he had a good imagination and that none of them had noticed.

But it looked like he wouldn't have to use his imagination anymore.

Justin was relieved to see Yedley was relaxing. He'd been afraid Justin wouldn't want him because of what had happened when Pryderi had come out. Justin could understand it, especially since Pryderi was his best friend, but he hadn't lied when he'd said the past didn't matter. He knew Pryderi wouldn't have agreed to have his brother move in with him and his mate if Yedley hadn't changed.

"I'm glad we talked about this. Is there anything else on your mind?" he asked.

Yedley chuckled. "Of course there is. But we just realized we were mates, and I'm a mess."

Justin could understand that. One part of him wanted to rush into this and pull Yedley in his arms, but he knew not to do that, not yet. "Take your time. We should probably go back upstairs before your brother eats our lunch, but I'm going to give you my phone number. I live in Whitedell, but I can shimmer here if you ever need me."

Yedley cocked his head. "Or I could shimmer to you. You're not a Nix."

"You're right, of course. I'm a werewolf. But I have several Nix friends, including your brother, so I'm sure I could find a way here if you need me."

"I don't think it will be necessary, but I won't say no to your phone number. Pryderi has been pushing me to accept a phone from him, and the main reason I haven't yet is that I wouldn't have had anyone to call."

Right. Yedley had lived with the tribe until just before he'd been kidnapped, and a lot of the tribes still lived without any modern comforts, including cell phones. Besides, even if Yedley's parents did have a phone, Justin doubted Yedley would have wanted to call them.

This really was a new start for him, and Justin wanted to make things easy for him. "I'm sure you'll make friends soon."

Yedley shrugged. "I already have a friend."

Pryderi had told Justin how close Yedley and Calvin were. Justin wasn't jealous, and he'd understand if Yedley didn't want to have more people in his life, but he didn't want Yedley to limit himself only because he was afraid. It would take time, but hopefully, Yedley would be able to settle in Gillham.

Which meant Justin had to start thinking about where he was going to live.

He didn't have family in Whitedell. He'd been assigned there, and he loved all his team members, but his best friend was moving away, and now his mate was in Gillham, too. Justin would miss his other friends, of course, but it seemed like everything was pushing him toward Gillham, and he didn't want to resist. He wanted to be there for Pryderi and Yedley if they needed him. He had time to think, of course, but he was pretty sure he'd already made his decision.

"I look forward to getting to know him, too," Justin said.

Yedley grimaced. "Calvin usually keeps to himself."

"I understand. Why don't we go back upstairs to have lunch?" Justin wanted more time alone with Yedley, but he was hungry, and he felt like they needed a break. Things had gone serious very fast. Actually, they'd started serious and had stayed that way. They needed some time to breathe and be themselves without those heavy topics on their minds.

Pryderi, Nate, and Calvin were still at the kitchen table when Justin and Yedley got back. Calvin kept looking around as if he expected someone to jump him, so Justin made sure to take the chair further away from him. Yedley, on the other hand, sat next to Calvin and leaned closer to him to whisper something in his ear. Calvin didn't react the way he might have if Yedley had told him Justin was his mate, so Justin suspected that whatever Yedley had said, it had nothing to do with him.

"You came back just in time. Pryderi was about to eat your sandwich," Nate teased.

Pryderi glared at him, but Justin could see he wasn't angry. It made Justin wonder if this was what he and Yedley would eventually have. He hoped so. This wouldn't be the first relationship he had, but it would be the last.

Justin wasn't going to fool himself into thinking he and Yedley wouldn't eventually bond. He knew they would. He knew resisting would be useless. He and Yedley shared a bond, and there was a reason for that bond. Justin would never find another man as perfect for him as Yedley was, and he wouldn't let Yedley slip from between his fingers. It was going to take work, but Justin was ready to do it. He'd seen enough bonded couples to know it was worth it.

"I wasn't," Pryderi protested.

They were both smiling, and Pryderi leaned closer to Nate, kissing his cheek—and snatching a few chips from his plate. He put them in his mouth smugly, then stuck his tongue out at his mate. "That'll teach you to make fun of me."

This was *exactly* what Justin wanted.

He stayed silent for the rest of the meal, listening to Nate and Pryderi and observing Calvin and Yedley. It was obvious Yedley was close to Calvin, and Justin imagined that what they'd been through had a lot to do with that. They'd been there for each other when no one else had been, and Justin suspected that meant that Calvin would be part of his life. He didn't have anything against that. He wanted Yedley to feel comfortable with him, and that meant accepting his family and his friends.

Pryderi waited until lunch was over to corner Justin. Justin had expected it, which was why he'd insisted on washing the dishes. It would give him and Pryderi a chance to use the empty kitchen for their conversation. Justin didn't know what Pryderi thought about him being his brother's mate. He hoped Pryderi would be okay with it, but he also expected his best friend to warn him to be careful. Pryderi loved both Justin and Yedley, and he wanted both of them to be happy.

Pryderi leaned against the counter next to the sink where Justin was washing the dishes. "So you're my brother's mate."

"I am."

"What happened downstairs? Did you and Yedley talk?"

"You know we did. That's why you sent us there. You wanted us to have a chance to talk things out before we had lunch."

"I want to know what you talked about. Come on."

"Why don't you ask your brother?" Justin didn't know if Yedley would be comfortable with him telling Pryderi about their conversation.

Pryderi rolled his eyes. "I will. But I'm asking *you* right now, and I want *you* to answer."

"Are you going to threaten to kick my ass if I hurt your brother?"

"Of course not. I know you won't. You're my best friend." He hesitated. "I'm not sure where I stand with Yedley. I'm happy he's here, of course, and even happier that he won't go back to the tribe and that he accepts me as I am, but we've been apart for so long. We were close when we were kids, but I'm not sure what we are now. I don't want to hurt him by asking him what happened, but sometimes, I'm not sure how to behave with him, you know?"

Pryderi was being cautious. It made sense that didn't know how to behave around his brother. "We talked about the past, mostly. He wanted me to know what he did to you. He thought I'd reject him once I found out."

Pryderi blinked. "What he did to me? You mean when he didn't stand up for me when I told my parents I was gay?"

"Exactly that. He thinks he's a coward for not telling your parents to stop. He thought it would be a deal-breaker for me, I guess."

"Because you're my best friend."

"In part."

"And is it a deal-breaker?"

"It's not. I told him the past is the past and that what he does now is more important than what he did then. I hope you're okay with it—I hope you're okay with me and your brother being mates."

Pryderi punched Justin's shoulder. "Of course I'm okay with it. I couldn't have asked for a better man for my brother. I know you'll treat him right and that you'll do everything you can to make him happy. That's all I've ever wanted for him."

Justin was relieved. He hadn't realized how important Pryderi's blessing was to him, but now that he had it, he could start thinking about his future with Yedley.

Chapter Two

"You seem more worried than I thought you'd be," Pryderi said.

Yedley turned and rolled his eyes. "How worried did you think I'd be? I met my mate. I don't know what to do with him, or with the rest of my life. I still haven't told our parents that I'm alive, or that I'm gay. I'm living with my brother even though I'm an adult."

Pryderi huffed and flopped onto the window seat next to Yedley. "Okay, you win. You have all the reasons in the world to be worried. I hate seeing you like this, though."

Yedley sighed. "I hate feeling this way, too." He should be happy. He had a new life, and that life included the brother he'd thought he'd lost and a mate. He could do whatever he wanted.

Yet he was moping and staring out the window because he didn't know what to do.

Even though he had a new beginning, he still felt that guilt about the past. He wasn't sure why that was, or what to do about it.

"What's wrong? I know we haven't been close in years, but you can talk to me," Pryderi said.

Anyone else would have kicked Yedley to the curb after what he'd done, but not Pryderi. Instead of doing that, he'd welcomed Yedley into his life and his apartment, and he hadn't protested once at having his and Nate's privacy invaded.

"I should be happy that I'm free and that I can do what I

want now, but I still feel uneasy, like there's something I need to do."

Pryderi hummed. "You never told me what happened when you were kidnapped."

"That's because there's not much to say."

"You don't have to talk about it, but I suspect it's part of the reason you feel unsettled."

Yedley didn't know if Pryderi was right, but he supposed it was worth a try. "I was in town."

"Wait, in *town*? Why were you in town? Who allowed you to go?"

Yedley glared. "Will you let me finish? You were the one who wanted to hear the story."

"Go ahead. Sorry."

Yedley understood why Pryderi was so shocked. Nix tribes had been modernizing ever since shifters were outed to the humans, but not all of them, and not at the same pace. The tribe where Pryderi and Yedley had grown up was one of those who wanted to stay isolated. They didn't like humans, and they liked shifters even less. They thought they needed to keep to themselves, so the fact that Yedley had been in town *was* strange.

"As I said, I was in town. Our parents didn't want me to go, but Mom was sick, and I wanted to buy her medicine. It was nothing bad, just a cold, but she'd been sick for weeks, and I thought it was worth it. I was walking along the sidewalk when someone pulled me into an alley and pushed me into a van. That's it."

"That must have been terrifying."

"It was. I'd hoped our parents would contact you when they realized I wasn't coming back, but they didn't, obviously."

"I'm sorry. I know it's disappointing."

Yedley shrugged. "Not really. I mean, I hoped they could

get over what they think of you for my sake, but it's obvious I'm not as important to them as their grudge. I should have known, and I'm learning to live with it." It wasn't like Yedley's parents would be in his life anyway. They would pitch a fit when he told them he was gay, which was one of the reasons he hadn't gone home yet. He already knew how they'd react, and it wouldn't be fun.

"Do you think that's why you can't relax yet?"

"What do you mean?"

"Well, it's unresolved business."

"I'm not a ghost."

Pryderi chuckled. "I realize that, and I'm thankful for it. But what I meant is that maybe you can't start your new life because you haven't entirely left the old one behind. You haven't been back to the tribe since you were taken. Your life was cut short, and I think it would be a good idea for you to go back."

Yedley shook his head. "I don't want to go."

"Trust me, I understand that. But you need closure with our parents, and probably to pick up your things. You're moving here permanently, right?"

"Of course I am. I know I should start looking for my own apartment, but—"

Pryderi reached out and squeezed Yedley's hand. "You can stay here for as long as you want to. Nate and I talked about it, so don't worry."

"You're newly mated. You shouldn't have to put up with me."

"We're not putting up with you. I love having you around, even though we're still finding our way in this brother relationship. And Nate is over the moon that your presence makes Calvin feel more at home and comfortable. I think he's a bit lost when it comes to his brother. They haven't seen each other for a long time, and he thought Calvin was dead."

Yedley knew that Calvin felt more comfortable with him than with Nate or Pryderi, but it made sense. Yedley might not have been in the cage the Beasts kept him in for as long as Calvin, but it had been enough for him and Calvin to talk and become close friends. Yedley didn't want to move out partly because of Calvin—and partly because the thought of living on his own was terrifying.

He'd never been on his own. He'd always lived with his parents and Pryderi, then with just his parents. Then he'd been in a cage, and now, here he was.

And he desperately wanted to feel comfortable. He wanted more than he had now. He just didn't know how to get it.

"I could come with you," Pryderi suggested, and it took Yedley a moment to understand what he was talking about because there was no way Pryderi *wanted* to go back.

When he did, he shook his head. "They won't let me in if they see you. I wish you could come, but I don't think it's a good idea." Both because their parents would pitch a fit, and because Pryderi shouldn't have to face them again, not after what they'd done.

"That means you'll go?"

Yedley didn't think he had a choice. As much as he wanted to stay away from the tribe and act like it was part of another life that wasn't his, it wasn't, not really. Pryderi was right. Yedley needed to get his things. He didn't have much, but it was his, and he wanted it back. "I guess I will." His parents would go crazy when he came out to them, so maybe he should wait until he was leaving to let them know.

Pryderi squeezed Yedley's hand again. "Don't tell them you're gay. I know you don't want to lose them, and even though I don't understand it, I don't *need* to understand."

"It's not because of that. At this point, I don't care if I lose them. But if I don't tell them I'm gay, they'll push for me to stay and get married as soon as possible. I won't come up with an excuse to avoid that. It wouldn't be fair to Justin, or to me."

Yedley would tell them the truth. He'd been planning to before he was kidnapped, but he hadn't had the time. He did now, even though he wished he didn't have to face them alone.

But he knew that if they saw Pryderi, they wouldn't listen. Yedley needed enough time to go inside the hut, pack his things, and get out. It wouldn't take long, although it depended on how his parents reacted to seeing him. He had no way to let them know he was okay other than going there and talking to them. They didn't have a phone or anything like that.

No, he would have to go there, no matter how much he wished he could avoid it.

"It might not be fair, but if you're not planning to go back, it might help. You don't owe them anything, not even the truth, not if you feel uncomfortable with it."

"I won't hide who I am." Yedley was done with that. The only reason he'd been hiding was that he only had his parents, but even that had only lasted so long. Yedley would rather be alone than having to lie, or worse, having to get married to make his parents happy.

He wasn't looking forward to it, but he knew what he had to do. It didn't matter that he had to do it alone. He was used to that.

****

This was weird. Justin had expected it when he'd requested to be transferred to Gillham, but still. He hadn't had a new team since he'd first become an enforcer. He still wasn't sure he'd move here indefinitely, but there was a good possibility he would. He and Yedley might only be trying to find their way around each other for now, but eventually, they'd be forever. Justin didn't want to take Yedley away from his brother, and he hadn't been looking forward to leaving his best friend behind, either. He didn't make friends easily, so the thought was slightly terrifying.

But this was work, and Justin was used to it. It wasn't the first meeting he went to, and it wouldn't be the last. He didn't know if this team would become his, but there was a good chance it would, and he wanted to be part of it.

"How many empty buildings are in town?" a woman asked.

Justin was pretty sure she'd introduced herself when she'd first walked in, but he had no idea what her name was. He was terrible with names.

"We don't have an exact number, unfortunately," Bran said.

Him, Justin remembered, since he was the head of the enforcers here in Gillham. He'd had to confirm Justin's transfer, and he'd been the one to decide which team Justin would fit better in.

"How are we supposed to visit all of them, then?"

"You're not the only team I'm putting on this. It's true that it will take a lot of time, but we need to make sure the Beasts are gone from town."

"It was too easy," a man grumbled. He was huge, and if Justin remembered well, his name was Xander. The only reason Justin did remember was that Xander was unforgettable. He wasn't quite seven feet tall, but he had to be close, and he was built like a brick house.

Bran nodded at him. "You're right, it was. I might be able to get behind that member of the Beasts telling us what he knows, because he found out one of their prisoners was his mate, but it doesn't feel right. There's more to it, and we have to find it. Unfortunately, so far, the moles we have in the gang haven't been able to tell us anything. They're trying, of course, but I don't want us just to sit around waiting for them to help. We need to make sure there are no Beasts left in town, and since they have a preference for empty buildings, the best thing we can do is go into every one of them and make sure they're empty."

Another man groaned. "So we're going to have to spend our days walking around town?"

"You are. Be careful, because we have no idea if the Beasts are really gone, and don't forget to write a report at the end of the day."

The man groaned louder. "I hate paperwork."

Xander reached out and patted the man's thigh. "Everyone hates paperwork, Davis."

Davis straightened. "How much do you want to do mine?"

Xander barked out a laugh. "I'm not doing your paperwork. I'm going home to my mate as soon as I can."

Davis slumped again. "Sure, rub it in our faces that you're mated."

Xander shook his head. He looked amused, and the way the two men were talking to each other reminded Justin of his old team. It might feel weird, but he had hopes he'd eventually get used to them. This team was obviously a family, the same way Justin's team had been, and it would take him a while to get to know them and to become part of it, but he could do this. Having Pryderi and Yedley in town would help, too.

"I'm not rubbing anything," Xander said.

"Except Muirgeh's—"

Xander slapped a hand on Davis' mouth. "Don't say it. I don't want to kick your ass, but I will if I need to."

"I was joking."

"I know. That's the only reason you still have all your teeth."

Bran cleared his throat. "If you're done playing around,

you have work to do. The sooner you get out there and start, the sooner you'll be home to your mates."

"That's not fair," Davis whined. "Only Xander and Sue are mated."

"Then you should start looking for your mate harder than you've been until now," Xander said as he got up.

Justin had to look up, and up, and *up* to get to his face. He'd always thought he was decently tall at six foot one, but he felt tiny next to Xander. He followed the team outside, feeling left out but understanding why.

"I think we should keep Xander away from the neighbors," Davis said. "He'll scare them."

Xander crossed his arms over his chest and glared at Davis, and Justin had to agree with him. He could tell Xander wasn't a bad man, but he'd had the occasion to spend a few hours with the man and the rest of the team. People who'd never seen him would probably be afraid, and while it sucked, it wasn't something they could change.

Sue rolled her eyes. "You can go, then, Davis."

Davis gaped. "I don't want to talk to the neighbors."

"Maybe not, but you just said we shouldn't send Xander, and I agree with you. He can be intimidating when he wants to be, and even when he doesn't. So the job is all yours. Take Rose with you so she can keep an eye on you."

"Why am I being punished?" a woman who had to be Rose asked. "I didn't do anything."

"You're right, you didn't, but you need to keep him in check. Who knows what he'll tell the neighbors? We need answers, not for them to call the cops on him."

Justin shook his head, unable not to smile. He would fit right in if he was given a chance, and he hoped he would.

"How is your first day going?" Sue asked as they headed out.

"Slightly overwhelming, but I expected it."

She nodded. "For what it's worth, I think you'll be a good fit. As I'm sure you realized, we can do with some quiet elements in our team."

"Where are we headed first?" Justin didn't know Gillham well. He'd spent most of his time in Gillham at the bar, but he was looking forward to seeing more of it. It was quaint, as pretty as Whitedell. They both had that small-town charm, which Justin didn't mind, and they were a mix of humans and shifters that appealed to him.

"There's a series of empty warehouses at the edge of town. Bran thinks it's a good idea to start there, since the Beasts needed space for their prisoners and their drugs. If they're all empty, we'll continue with the empty houses that are sprinkled around town."

Justin wasn't looking forward to exploring empty buildings, but he was relieved that the team was welcoming him. He wanted this to work because he wanted to be close to Pryderi and Yedley.

As he'd thought, the day was boring. They managed to search through three warehouses, which was a high number for such a small town, or at least, Justin thought so. He wasn't the one who gave orders, though, so he followed Sue's lead. The buildings were all empty, and while it had been boring as hell, he was relieved. It meant there wasn't much paperwork to complete, and *that* meant he could go to the bar early. He was eager to see Yedley.

They hadn't talked much yet. Justin was trying to give Yedley space and time because he wasn't sure what else he could do. He'd had relationships before, but none of them had been as important as this one, or as important as it would be eventually. Justin didn't want to mess things up. Maybe he should talk to Pryderi and ask him how Yedley was and what he could do to make him feel better, but he wasn't sure how well that would go down with Yedley.

The bar was closed when Justin got there, but Nate had told him he was welcome anytime. He didn't have a key, but he knew that at this time of the day, someone was bound to be at the bar since they were getting ready for the evening customers. He quickly knocked on the door before pushing it open and slipping in, making sure to close it behind him.

He was surprised to see Yedley of all people behind the bar. Yedley looked up, his mouth open, and froze before words could come out of it.

****

Yedley was washing glasses when he heard the door open. Since the bar was still closed, he looked up to tell the customer to leave, but he didn't say anything because he recognized the man standing there.

He hadn't expected to see Justin today. He'd been psyching himself up to shimmer to the tribe and talk to his parents, and he'd been thinking about it for most of the day. No matter how hard he'd tried to distract himself, it hadn't worked. He needed to do something different, but he didn't know where to start.

Maybe Justin would distract Yedley. Of course, Yedley would have to unfreeze himself first.

He swallowed and put down the glass. "I didn't expect you."

"I can go if you want me to."

Yedley shook his head. "Stay, please." He *wanted* Justin to stay, but he didn't know how to admit it.

This was harder than Yedley had thought. He'd never cared much about the women he'd dated. He'd been with them more because of his parents than because he wanted to, but this was different.

Justin stepped away from the door and gestured at the counter. "Mind if I keep you company?"

"Of course not. I can give you a drink if you want, but don't ask for beer, because I have no idea how the beer thingie works."

Justin chuckled. "A soda is fine."

He was still wearing his uniform, and he looked good in it. He watched Yedley as Yedley got one of the sodas out of the fridge and poured it into the glass. Yedley could feel his gaze on him, and it made him feel flustered. Clearly, having Justin with him *was* a good distraction.

Yedley placed the soda in front of Justin, and when Justin reached for his pocket, he shook his head. "It's on me."

"You don't have to do that."

"I know I don't. It's a thank you for the company until the bar opens."

"I'm more than happy to give you company. I'm surprised to find you working."

Yedley shrugged and went back to his dirty glasses. "I'm trying to earn my keep."

Justin frowned. "I don't think Pryderi expects you to do anything like that. He's happy to have you with him."

"I know he is. I just feel like I'm not doing enough. Pryderi gave me a home. I have a roof over my head and food in my stomach thanks to him. I should do more to thank him and to contribute, you know? Especially since Calvin still isn't leaving the apartment."

"You should probably talk to your brother about this."

Yedley had already talked to Pryderi, and Pryderi hadn't managed to make him change his mind. Yedley needed to contribute, and he was more than ready to do it. He wasn't sure how yet, but helping at the bar was a start. "This is fine. I'm happy to do this. It gives me less time to think."

Justin arched a brow. "Less time to think? Is something

wrong? Or are you just trying to avoid thinking about me?"

Yedley didn't want to blush, but like all Nix, his skin was pale enough that there was no way Justin would miss the flush. "I'm not. I swear. But I decided to go visit my parents so I can pack my things and finish moving in with Pryderi, and it's not something I'm eager to think about. They won't be happy, not when I explain I'm moving out."

Yedley snapped his mouth shut. He didn't mean to babble, yet here he was.

"Is Pryderi going with you?"

"No. He wanted to, but the situation is already going to be hard enough as it is. Adding Pryderi to the mix won't help. If anything, it will make things worse. My parents don't think of him as their son anymore, and they'll lose it if he as much as goes close to the tribe."

"I could come with you."

Yedley blinked. That was an even worse idea than having Pryderi with him, but for some reason, he couldn't find it in himself to say no. "Why would you want to come? Trust me, my parents aren't the kind of people you want to be friends with."

"I don't want to be friends with them. But you're going, and you could do with some support. Since you don't want your brother there, I'd like to come, if it's okay with you. I know we're not close or anything, but you're my mate, and I want you to be happy. I want to protect you and be there for you."

Yedley wanted to say yes. He didn't think he could face his parents on his own, and if he couldn't have Pryderi with him, Justin would be a perfect choice, at least from Yedley's point of view.

But Yedley didn't want Justin to meet his parents. They were horrible people who hadn't thought twice about kicking their son out because of who he loved. They were going to make a scene, and even though Yedley wasn't planning on having any kind of contact with them after he talked to them, he still didn't want Justin to see them for what they were.

He didn't want Justin to think badly of him because of his parents.

He realized that the way his parents behaved had nothing to do with him, even after the way he'd behaved when Pryderi had come out to them. He'd known it was wrong, and he'd learned from that mistake. *They* hadn't, though. They still thought Pryderi was somehow wrong because he was in love with Nate, and Nate was a man.

He cleared his throat. "They won't be happy once I tell them I'm gay."

"You'll tell them?"

"Of course I will. If I don't, they'll expect me to stay with the tribe and get married. Besides, even if they don't, I won't hide anymore. It hurt Pryderi, and me, too. Neither of us deserves to keep a part of ourselves hidden just because our parents can't deal with it. I want to be myself. I never thought I'd have the chance, but the time I spent here in Gillham showed me I was wrong. I can be myself and be happy. I can have what everyone else has—a family, a mate, a job. Who I love doesn't change that."

"You don't have to tell them I'm your mate if I go with you, though. I wouldn't mind. I understand how hard dealing with families can be."

"How did your family react when you told them you liked guys?" Or had he? Yedley didn't know much about Justin yet. He wanted to find out, but he didn't know how.

"There were okay with it. My mom said she suspected since I was a teenager, but I don't know about that. I don't care, either. As long as they accept me, I'm okay. That doesn't mean there wasn't drama, which is why I said I understand how hard it can be, but it was nothing like what your parents did."

"I'm not willing to hide you." Even though Justin was right when he said it would make things easier. Yedley's parents would freak out when he came out. If he dragged his mate there and introduced them, things would be even harder.

Yedley's parents would kick them out. Yedley was sure of it. Maybe he could wait to tell them until he was packed and on his way out. They'd try to stop him, but hopefully, Justin's presence would confuse them for long enough.

To Yedley's surprise, Justin reached over the bar and grabbed his hand. "You wouldn't be hiding me. Does what your parents think count for you? You said yourself that you're not planning to see them ever again once this is over."

"That's why I want to tell them. I want them to know why I'm leaving. I want them to know the reason they lost both their sons. They'll never realize it was because of their behavior otherwise. Besides, you don't deserve to be hidden. I'm not ashamed of the bond between us."

"You wouldn't be doing it because you're ashamed. Keeping the peace can be as important as being honest." Justin squeezed Yedley's hand and leaned back.

Yedley wanted to touch him again, but instead, he focused on the glasses.

"But you know your parents better than I do, so I'll follow your lead."

"Does that mean you're still coming?" Yedley prayed he was, even though he'd been trying to convince him otherwise.

"Of course I am, unless you don't want me to. I told you, I want to support you since your brother can't."

Yedley allowed himself to breathe. Things would be okay. He wouldn't have to face his parents alone, and once that was over, he'd come back to his real family and live the life he'd always dreamed of.

****

Justin wouldn't have minded it if Yedley had decided to hide the truth from his parents, but he was relieved he wouldn't.

Justin didn't want to be a secret. He would have accepted it if that was the way Yedley wanted it, since he knew his parents and Justin didn't, but he felt better. He was still uneasy about facing Yedley's parents, mostly because they sounded like assholes, but he'd do it. He wanted to be Yedley's rock, the person Yedley leaned on when he needed help, or even when he only needed a shoulder to cry on.

"You shouldn't care about what your parents think," Justin said even though he knew how hard that could be. He had no idea how it felt to be in Yedley's position. His parents had been nonplussed when Justin had told him he liked guys better than girls, but they'd accepted it easily enough. He'd never had to fear they would get angry and kick him out.

"I don't, not really."

To Justin, it looked like Yedley cared a lot about what his parents would think, but he could be wrong.

Yedley leaned against the counter toward Justin. "I can see you don't believe me. But it's true. I don't care what they think about me. I realized a long time ago that they'll think I'm disgusting once I tell them, and I've had time to get used to that. But I'm not looking forward to telling them I'm gay and having to stand there while they pitch a fit. Honestly, I wouldn't go if Pryderi didn't think it was a good idea."

"Why does he think that?"

"I was telling him that I feel like there's something stopping me from fully enjoying this new life. I'm not sure what it is, but Pryderi is convinced that I have to leave the past behind and that I won't be able to do that until I face our parents. He said it was unfinished business."

"He's aware you're not a ghost, right?"

Yedley chuckled. "That's what I told him. But I don't know. Maybe he's right. It *is* true that I didn't leave because I chose to. I was taken away, and maybe I have to face that. Besides, I want to get my things back. It's not a lot, but it's mine, and I think it might help me feel more at home here."

That was what Justin wanted. Gillham was a new start for both of them, and he wanted things to work. "Well, like I said, I'll be there with you."

Yedley grimaced. "Maybe you shouldn't come. I want you to, but it won't be nice. My parents are going to freak out, and that's when the insults start flying. I'd rather not have you listen to that."

"I've been through worse. I've been an enforcer for years, and there is no way meeting your parents will be worse than that. I can stand a few insults and rumblings." Justin hesitated. "Unless you think they'll do worse?"

Yedley frowned. "What do you mean?"

"Could it become physical?"

Yedley blinked. "Physical? You mean, are they going to become violent?"

"Yes." Justin's parents might have been okay with him being gay, but he'd seen plenty of homophobic people react badly. He didn't want Yedley to get hurt, which was one more reason his presence there would be a good idea.

"I don't think so. They're not physical people. They're assholes, and they'll scream at us, but no. I don't think they'll try to hit us."

Justin was relieved. He'd been ready to protect Yedley if he needed to, but he'd rather not have to arrest his parents. They might never see them again after that day, but they were still Yedley's parents. It wouldn't be the best start in their relationship if Justin had to beat their asses. "When do you want to go? I just started working with the enforcers here, but I'm sure I can take a few days off." It wasn't like Sue needed him to search the empty warehouses and houses. The three they'd visited today had been empty, and Justin suspected the next ones would be, too.

"I don't think we'll need days. An afternoon, maybe? I'll shimmer us there, we'll grab my stuff, I'll tell them I'm gay, and we'll be out of there."

"How about you take at least a day afterward to relax and process everything?" Even though Yedley expected his parents to take this badly, Justin couldn't imagine it was an easy thing to accept and deal with. They were still Yedley's parents, no matter how badly they behaved.

Yedley looked around. "I should help Nate and Pryderi."

"Pryderi won't mind, and neither will Nate. They both understand this isn't an easy situation for you, and you've been through a lot in the past few months."

"I don't know. I have no idea what I'd do with two days. I'm not really into relaxing right now."

"That's because you haven't tried. Come on. You know you need it. I'm sure I can organize something and spend those few days with you. We can talk, grow closer hopefully."

"It *is* true we haven't had much time together."

That was mostly Justin's fault. He'd been busy going back to Whitedell to talk to his team leader and have her contact Bran. Then he'd had to pack some of his stuff and move to Gillham, start working and getting to know his new team. There had been a lot of paperwork and not nearly enough time with Yedley.

Justin wanted to change that. He wanted to be there for Yedley, but he also wanted them to get to know each other. He could feel the bond between them, wanting them to move closer, and his werewolf was on board with that. But it was complicated to deal with a new relationship while also dealing with everything else, so a few days away from Gillham and the enforcers sounded good. It wouldn't be the best of occasions, but it was better than nothing, and Justin suspected Yedley really would need some time to get over what would happen with his parents.

"Let me talk to my team leader," Justin said. He wanted to reach for Yedley's hand again, but he wasn't sure Yedley would allow it, and he wasn't about to crowd his mate. "I'll ask her if I can take a few vacation days, possibly tomorrow and the day after that. We can talk with your parents and get that out of the way tomorrow morning, then maybe shimmer to a beach somewhere and have fun before we have to come back."

"Where would we sleep?"

Justin thought Yedley sounded interested. "We'll get a hotel. Let me know if you have a place you always wanted to visit and haven't been yet, and I'll make a few calls and find a room."

"I don't know. I've never really thought about it. Even when I decided I wanted to leave the tribe, the only place I could think about living in was Gillham because Pryderi is here. The tribe has always isolated itself, and that goes for me, too. To be honest, the thought of being able to go wherever I want is daunting."

Justin stopped resisting. He put his hand on the counter with his palm up in what he hoped was a clear invitation. Yedley's gaze flicked from Justin's face to his hand, and he pressed his own palm against it.

Justin relaxed and turned his hand over so they could hook their fingers together. "We don't have to do this if you don't want to, but I still think it would be nice. Or we could come back here and spend two days in your bedroom. To talk, of course," he added in a rush.

Yedley laughed. "I don't think my brother would be happy if we did that. Maybe you're right. I'm just afraid I won't be the best company after we leave the tribe."

Justin squeezed Yedley's hand. "I don't expect you to be. That's one of the reasons I think we should get away for a few days. You'll have time to relax and sift through your feelings about what happened. It won't work miracles, but it will distract you, and that's what you'll need. If you don't want to choose, I will. I already have a few ideas."

Yedley nodded. "All right. I trust you."

Justin hadn't expected that, but he would make sure he didn't betray that trust. Their two days together would start badly, but nothing said they'd have to continue that way. This was their first trip together, and Justin would make it count.

CHAPTER THREE

Yedley wasn't surprised to see Justin was holding a bag, but it made his stomach churn weirdly. He had one too. His was only half full, though, and it didn't have the same meaning. He'd brought clothes and toiletries, but that was all he'd need, and he had to save empty space for the things he needed to pick up from his parents.

He wasn't looking forward to this, but he *was* looking forward to what would come after it.

If it were up to him, he'd never go back. He was tempted to tell Justin he'd shimmer them to whatever place Justin wanted to go to after and forget all about the tribe. He'd do just that if he didn't think Pryderi was right.

Yedley needed closure. He needed to be able to leave his old life behind, and that wouldn't happen until he faced his parents and his past. He might hate it, but he had to go through it.

Justin looked up and smiled at Yedley when Yedley stepped into the bar. He hadn't asked Justin to come up to the apartment because he suspected it would have been too easy to get distracted and stay there if he had. Justin was here because he wanted to support Yedley through his meeting with his parents, not because he wanted to spend two days with Yedley. Or maybe he did, but the main reason was to go to the tribe, and that was what Yedley would do.

"Ready?" Justin asked.

Yedley grimaced. "I don't think I'll ever be ready to face my parents."

Justin's smile fell a bit, and Yedley hated himself for doing that. He didn't want to lie to his mate, though. It wouldn't be a great start to their relationship.

"I won't tell you everything will be okay because I have no way to know if that is the case, but I'll be there for you."

Yedley already knew that, but he was grateful for the reminder. "Thank you. I don't think I'd be able to do this if you hadn't volunteered to come with me." It was more that Yedley would have avoided doing it entirely, but Justin was aware of that. They'd talked about it yesterday, after all.

They both turned around at the sound of someone else coming into the bar. Yedley wasn't surprised to see his brother. He'd snuck out of the apartment because he'd known Pryderi would try to talk to him before he left, and he wasn't sure he could go through that. He didn't know if Pryderi would try to stop him, but he wouldn't risk it. This might have been Pryderi's idea, but Yedley knew how uncomfortable Pryderi was with it.

Pryderi's expression relaxed when he saw Yedley was still there. "Good. I wanted to catch you before you left."

Yep. He was there to try to convince Yedley to stay. He wanted the best for Yedley, and Yedley would get hurt if he talked to their parents. Pryderi had already gone through it, so he knew what it would be like.

"I'm going. You were right. I need to go through this to leave the past behind and focus on the future," Yedley said before his brother could add anything.

Pryderi sighed. "I knew you would say that. Once you decide something, you don't back down. But I wanted you to know that you don't *have* to do this. It won't be easy. I know that."

"And that's exactly why I should do it. If I don't, I'll always wonder what our parents think about my disappearance. I'll always wonder if they care, if they worry. I don't want to start my new life wondering about my past. I need to be a hundred percent sure they won't accept me, even though I already know they won't." Yedley shook his head. "I know it doesn't make sense."

"It does. You already know they won't want you in their life if you tell them you're gay, but you need to be sure of it. You need them to say it to you to your face." Pryderi hugged Yedley, and Yedley buried his face against his brother's neck. "I'll be here for you when you come back. You can tell me to fuck off, or we can watch movies, or whatever. But remember that I've been through this, and I know how it feels."

Maybe Justin's idea of going away after wasn't a bad one. Yedley would need to be distracted. He appreciated Pryderi's offer to talk, but he wasn't sure he'd be in the mood. No matter that he already knew what would happen, it wouldn't be easy, and he wouldn't want to think about it more than he had to.

Pryderi stepped back, trailing his hand down Yedley's arm and quickly squeezing his hand before letting go entirely. "I'm here for you. I know I'm not the only one, but I want you to know that."

Yedley's chest felt tight. For so long, he'd thought he'd lost his brother. He didn't know how Pryderi had worked through his feelings and had managed to still care for Yedley after what he'd done, but he was glad for it. He'd always have his brother, and he'd always have Justin, at least if he played this right. "Thanks for saying it."

"I'll tell you any time you need to be reminded of it. You should probably go before I try to change your mind again. I hate the thought of you getting hurt, and I don't want you to have to go through this."

Yedley nodded and stepped closer to Justin. He offered Justin his hand, and he was surprised when his mate didn't even hesitate. He was probably used to shimmering since he was an enforcer, but still. Shimmering always put him in the hands of the Nix doing it. Yedley could take Justin wherever he wanted, and Justin wouldn't be able to stop him. The fact that Justin seemed to trust him entirely and without hesitation was another thing that touched Yedley.

Yedley wasn't alone. He'd thought he would be when he left the tribe, and maybe he would have been. He didn't know what had changed the outcome, if it was getting kidnapped or something else, but it didn't matter. He had his brother, and he had his mate. He had a best friend, and Pryderi's mate, too. It was a small family, but they cared for him, and that meant it was better than anything else he'd ever had.

Yedley linked his fingers with Justin's and looked at his brother. Pryderi nodded, even though he looked worried, and Yedley shimmered away with that image in his mind. He didn't have to think of the tribe to shimmer there because he'd done this so many times over the years. Taking his brother's image with him made him feel better, and he didn't immediately feel the need to run when he and Justin appeared at the entrance of the tribe.

Yedley took a deep breath and looked around. He'd lived here his entire life. He hadn't known anything else until he'd been taken. But now that he had spent time in Gillham, he could see how awful the place was.

It was so isolated that it didn't have electricity or running water. The Nix lived in huts that were freezing in the winter and boiling in the summer. All of that had seemed normal to Yedley until he'd started living with Pryderi and Nate, but now he could see it wasn't. The tribe lost children because of how rustic the conditions where. People got sick and never recovered. They could change that if they reached out to the council, but they never had. Yedley hadn't been involved in how the tribe was led, but he knew the elders well enough to understand why they hadn't.

They risked losing control over the tribe members if they did. If the tribe members realized there was something more out there for them, a life that could be everything they wanted, they'd take it. If it meant leaving the tribe behind, Yedley didn't think any of them would hesitate.

The tribe had been his family all his life, but now he realized how bad a family it was. They used fear to keep people there. They hid the fact that they could have more. Yedley wished everyone would realize that, but he understood it was a pointless dream. He couldn't allow himself to feel sorry for the other tribe members. He couldn't allow himself to get stuck in the tribe for them. Maybe he could come back later, when he was stronger, and try to talk to them, to make them see there was more to the world than their corner of the woods, but not now. Not yet.

Justin didn't release Yedley's hand as they stepped toward the huts, and Yedley was grateful for that. He swallowed as a woman came out of her hut, saw them, and went immediately back inside.

They'd been noticed.

Justin had never thought about how Nix lived. The only Nix he knew where part of the pack or enforcers. They lived in houses and apartments.

The tribe didn't.

To say it was rustic was an understatement. The tribe consisted of a series of small huts gathered around a fire pit. It wasn't lit now, and no one was sitting around it. That didn't mean the place was empty, though. Apart from the woman who'd gone straight back into her hut, Justin noticed a few people peeking out of their doors. They seemed to find Yedley's presence fascinating, or maybe it was Justin's. Justin didn't know how isolated the tribe was, but from what he could see, they didn't have a lot of contact with the outside world. There were no signs of anything modern, and every-thing — including their clothes — seemed to be handmade. He had a hard time imagining Yedley in them.

He couldn't help but wonder if Yedley would miss this. It wasn't Justin's thing, since he liked his comforts, but that didn't mean Yedley hadn't been happy here. Apart from the problems with his parents, this was Yedley's home. Justin didn't know how his life had been until he'd been kidnapped. Maybe he had friends here. Maybe he had other family members who cared for him.

Justin didn't think Yedley would move back here, not with his brother in Gillham, but this was something to think about.

A little girl rushed out the door of a hut, and Justin smiled at her. Her eyes widened, but before anything could happen, her mother grabbed her and pulled her back inside. Justin sighed. He didn't like when people were afraid of him, and it was obvious that was the case here. The tribe didn't have a reason to fear him, but he doubted they'd take his word for it.

"They're not used to visitors," Yedley said in an apologetic tone.

"I suspected that."

"It's nothing against you in particular. They just don't like strangers."

Justin nodded as a man came around a hut and noticed them. His eyes went wide, and he rushed into one of the huts. Justin didn't miss the way Yedley winced. "What's going on?" he asked.

"That's my parents' place. He's telling them I'm back."

"Well, you knew you'd be noticed eventually. How long has it been since you were home?"

"Not long enough."

Justin would have laughed if he hadn't known Yedley was serious. He didn't have time to say anything, though, because a couple burst out of the hut and rushed toward them.

They both looked like Yedley. Justin could see the same eyes on Yedley and his mother, and the same shape of the jaw on him and his dad. The three of them had long blond hair and green eyes, but then, so did Pryderi. It was a distinctive sign of Nix.

Justin let go of Yedley's hand, not because he wanted to but because he wanted to give Yedley and his parents space. He knew Yedley expected this to go badly, but he still hoped Yedley was wrong and that his parents would accept him. They'd had to live with his disappearance and not knowing what had happened to him for a while. Hopefully, that had made them realize how much they cared for their son.

"Yedley!" Yedley's mother yelled. She threw herself at her son, but Yedley took a step back and shook his head.

His mother stumbled, obviously confused. She reached for Yedley again, but to Justin's relief, Yedley's father touched her shoulder and kept her back.

"Yedley?" Yedley's father asked.

"I think we should talk," Yedley said.

Justin winced. This probably wasn't what Yedley's parents expected. They hadn't even noticed him yet, but with Yedley being as cold as he was, it wouldn't take long.

"What happened to you? Where have you been? We've looked all over the forest, and we even went into town to make sure you weren't there," Yedley's mother said.

Yedley straightened his back. "Like I said, we need to talk, and I think we should do so in private."

Yedley's parents looked even more confused now, but they nodded and stepped back. Justin followed three of them toward their hut, trying to keep himself out of sight. He wouldn't let Yedley face this alone, but he knew that his presence would make everything more complicated for his mate, so the later Yedley's parents realized why he was there, the better it would be.

Justin was surprised to find a woman sitting in the hut when they walked in. He looked at Yedley, planning to follow his lead on this, but Yedley looked as baffled as Justin felt.

"We need to talk *alone*," Yedley said to his parents.

Justin pressed his back against the wall, trying to make himself invisible. He didn't know what was happening, and he didn't want to overstep. He'd be there for Yedley if Yedley needed him, but otherwise, he'd try to blend into the decor, which wouldn't be easy since the hut was mostly empty.

There was a wooden table with three chairs round it, all of it handmade. There was an opening that led to another room, but Justin couldn't see what room that was. There wasn't much else in the room, except a few covered baskets sat on a second table.

"But Dylana is family," Yedley's mother protested.

From Yedley's expression, Justin doubted that was true, at least to him. It was possible that Dylana had been there for Yedley's parents when Yedley had disappeared, but as far as Yedley was concerned, Justin didn't think she was important to him.

"*I* am family, and I need to talk to you alone," Yedley snapped.

"She was so worried for you. We all were."

"I understand that, but I don't want anyone but my closest family members here when I say what I have to say."

Yedley's father looked at Justin. Justin wasn't surprised he'd been noticed, of course. The only reason they hadn't said anything was because they'd been focused on their son, but that was bound to end, and it had. "Why is he here, then? You said you wanted to talk to family, and he's not part of it."

Yedley shook his head. "I'll tell you everything as soon as we're alone, I promise. But Justin isn't going anywhere." He looked at Dylana. "I'm sorry about this. I don't mean to throw you out, but I'm sure you understand that after being kidnapped and almost being experimented on, I want some time with my parents."

Dylana's eyes widened, and she stepped toward the door, but Yedley's mother stopped her. "She should stay. I know you and she hadn't talked about this, and that everything was messed up when you disappeared, but her parents had agreed for the two of you to get married before you left."

Yedley crossed his arms over his chest. "I didn't leave. I was kidnapped. I was almost experimented on in a lab. And I won't marry Dylana. I'm sorry, but it's out of the question."

Yedley's mother opened her mouth, but her husband once again put a hand on her arm. He shook his head. "We'll have time to talk about this later. Yedley needs some time alone, and since he said he was kidnapped, it's understandable. It's not like either he or Dylana are going anywhere. They'll have another opportunity to be together soon enough."

No one said anything about Justin staying. Justin was relieved. He didn't want to have to fight with Yedley's parents, and he would have to if they tried to kick him out. He wasn't going anywhere, not without Yedley.

Dylana left without saying a thing. To Justin, she looked relieved, which was probably an indication of the fact that she wanted to marry Yedley as much as Yedley wanted to marry her—which was not at all. The entire situation felt like a step back in time. Did people here really organize their children's marriages without asking them what they wanted?

Yedley's father closed the wooden door behind Dylana and turned to look at his son. "What's going on, Yedley? Why did you want to send Dylana away? I understand you've been through a lot, but she could have helped you."

Yedley looked at Justin, and Justin knew he needed him. He stepped closer, and to Justin's surprise, Yedley took his hand. He linked their fingers together and faced his parents

46

again.

Justin held his breath.

Yedley stood tall and strong as he said, "I wanted to talk to you alone because of this."

Yedley felt like he might throw up. He knew it was only in his mind, but he couldn't help it, not when he'd just come out to his parents.

Except they didn't seem to understand what was happening.

Yedley's mother frowned. "I don't understand. Why are you holding that man's hand? Who is he?"

At least she'd stopped trying to push Yedley and Dylana together. Yedley supposed he should be relieved, and he was, but he couldn't wait for this to be over.

"Don't you want to know what happened to me? How I got out? Do you even care?"

"Of course we care. We were frantic when you disappeared."

"Yet you didn't contact Pryderi."

"We couldn't."

"Of course you could, and you should have. He's an enforcer, but most importantly, he's my brother, and he deserved to know that something had happened to me." Yedley breathed in and out a few times. Yelling at his parents wouldn't solve anything. It wouldn't help, except making him feel slightly better.

"He's not our son anymore. You were there when he told us what he was. You have to understand that."

"I don't. Pryderi is still the same man he was before. Who he's mated to doesn't matter. It doesn't change him. You shouldn't have kicked him out, but you know what? I'm glad you did, because he wouldn't have become an enforcer otherwise, and he wouldn't have met his mate." And he wouldn't have been there when Yedley and Calvin had needed him.

Yedley wanted his parents to ask about Pryderi and Nate. He wanted them to care, but he wasn't surprised they didn't. They didn't even act like they'd heard what he'd said. They were focused on him, and Yedley knew it wouldn't take long for them to understand why Justin was there and why Yedley was still holding hands with him. The only reason they hadn't yet was that they were distracted by what Yedley as saying.

He needed to tell them. Waiting wouldn't change anything, and he had enough of walking on eggshells around them. If they had a problem with Justin and who he was to Yedley, it was *their* problem, not Yedley's. It was their own fault they were about to lose their second son.

Yedley faced his parents. "This is Justin. He's my mate, and I'm moving to Gillham to be with him and to build a better relationship with Pryderi."

Yedley had managed to shock his parents into silence, but it didn't last long. His mother started shrieking, and Yedley tuned her out. He could imagine all too well what she was saying anyway. Instead, he looked at his father.

Yedley knew his parents wouldn't take this well, but he hadn't been able to stop himself from hoping. He wasn't any different from Pryderi except for the fact that once Pryderi had left, his parents had focused on him. They expected him to get married, obviously to Dylana, and have children. They'd thought he'd always be around. He *could* be around, but that depended on them and how they reacted to the news that his mate was a man. It was obvious they wouldn't accept it, though. It hurt, but Yedley had worked through those feelings a long time ago.

"Can you stop yelling?" he snapped at his mother.

Talking to her that way must have shocked her—she

suddenly became silent. She looked at him with eyes that were so similar to his that he saw them every time he looked in a mirror.

He swallowed. "Yelling won't change anything. Justin is my mate, and yes, he's a man. I'm gay."

Yedley's father shook his head. "You said you wanted a relationship with your brother. Is he the one who put these thoughts in your mind?"

That, Yedley hadn't expected. "Of course not. I've always known I was gay. Pryderi has nothing to do with this."

"You didn't say anything before, though. You had relationships with women."

"Can you blame me for not telling you? You kicked Pryderi out when he did. You told me a few minutes ago that he wasn't your son anymore because of who he loves. Did you really expect me to tell you I was like him when I saw your reaction when he did?"

Yedley's father shook his head. "There has to be a mistake. You're our only son."

"No, I'm not. Either you have two sons, or you have none at all." Yedley cleared his throat. His eyes burned, but he wouldn't cry. He didn't want to show his parents how much he hurt over their reaction. "Anyway, the reason I'm here is to pack my things. Like I told you before, I'm moving to Gillham."

"You can't move."

"Of course I can. You're welcome to visit me if you want, but that probably won't happen. I won't abandon Justin. He's my mate, and that means something to me. I also won't stop talking to Pryderi. You should never have kicked him out, and I should have stood up for him. I hate myself for not doing so, but that's going to change. I'm standing up for him now, and I'm standing up for myself. You can either decide to have both of us in your life or neither of us." He didn't know if Pryderi wanted to talk to their parents again, but if Yedley could give him a possibility to do it if he did, it had to be a good thing, right?

"What did they do to you when they kidnapped you?" Yedley's mother asked. She sounded horrified, and it took Yedley a second to understand what she was asking.

He snorted. "Nothing. I told you, I was kidnapped, but they didn't have time to do anything to me. I was a prisoner for a while, but that's about it. I didn't become gay because of this. I was already gay years ago. The only reason I didn't tell you was that I knew you'd take it badly. I was scared, but I'm not anymore. I've been through worse, and I know I can survive this."

And he had Pryderi and Justin. He didn't think he'd be able to do this without them in his life.

"You can ignore the bond."

His mother was desperate, wasn't she? Yedley shook his head and pushed past his parents, dragging Justin along with him as he headed to the tiny room that had once been his bedroom. He had to pass through his parents' room to get there, and his own room was a tight fit since his parents followed him and Justin there, but at least he'd be able to shimmer right from there. He didn't have to go through the house he'd lived in all his life again. He didn't have to think about the memories anymore.

He would try not to, anyway.

"What do you want me to do?" Justin asked. He was Yedley's rock right now, a strong presence that told Yedley that everything would be okay no matter what happened.

"Just grab whatever you see and put it in my bag. Leave the clothes here, though. I won't need them."

Justin nodded and got to work. Unfortunately, that gave Yedley's parents more time to yell at him. "Meeting your mate doesn't mean you have to bond with him," Yedley's mother told him. "You can come home, and I'm sure Dylana won't mind. She'll understand."

"*You* don't understand. I have no intention of ignoring the bond between Justin and me. I want to be with him. Nothing you can do or say will change my mind about this, and that includes you kicking me out because I'm gay. I should have told you a long time ago. I was going to before I was kidnapped. And now you know, and you reacted exactly the way I thought you would." And he couldn't wait to get out of here. He *needed* to get out of here.

Yedley held his hand out to Justin, who thankfully was almost done. Justin pushed a few more things into Yedley's bag, then hauled it onto his shoulder and took Yedley's hand. He looked at Yedley's parents, a frown on his face. "I wish you could see how incredible your son is. Both of them. They're good men, and who they love doesn't change that. I wish you could see that, and I wish Yedley wasn't losing his family, but he has another one. He'll be fine. I'll make sure of it."

Yedley didn't want to fight anymore. He didn't want to hear his parents try to change his mind anymore. So he squeezed Justin's hand and shimmered them away.

Justin had no idea where they were when they arrived, but Yedley was shaking, so he focused on his mate. He could figure out where they were later, once Yedley felt better.

Justin wasn't sure what Yedley would allow, but he pulled his mate into his arms, holding his breath until he realized Yedley wouldn't push him away. He cuddled Yedley against his chest and kissed his hair, trying to make him understand he wasn't alone, no matter what had happened with his parents.

Justin was relieved when Yedley's arms wrapped around him, and he hugged back.

"Are you okay?" Justin asked, even though he knew it was a stupid question. Of course Yedley wasn't okay.

"I will be. Thank you for being there for me, though."

"Always. You don't even have to ask."

Yedley leaned back, and to Justin's relief, he was smiling. "That's good to know. But I know this can't have been easy for you."

"It wasn't as hard as it was for you. Really, Yedley, you don't have to worry about me." Maybe Justin should try to get Yedley to think about something else.

He finally looked around. Yedley had shimmered them in front of the bed-and-breakfast Justin had found. He'd been trying to choose a place that was romantic enough that things between him and Yedley might progress to the next level, whatever that level was, but not so romantic that it wouldn't work in case Yedley wanted to do nothing more than cry for the next two days. Whatever he needed, Justin was ready to give it to him, and he'd made sure the place was okay with Yedley by showing him pictures. "We can go home if you want. Maybe you should talk to your brother."

"There's nothing Pryderi can do. I already knew what was going to happen, so even though I'm sad, I'm not surprised. I was ready." He looked at the bed-and-breakfast. "This is a nice place."

It was. Justin had no idea what Yedley liked, but he loved the ocean, so he'd chosen a bed-and-breakfast close to the beach. It would be too cold to swim, but they could spend some time on the beach, or they could explore the small town the bed-and-breakfast was situated in. Justin had checked that downtown was in walking distance, and he hoped the small-town ambiance and the ocean would help Yedley relax and forget about his parents, even if it was only for a few days.

"We can do whatever you want."

Yedley nodded and stepped away. "Why don't we go in?

We can leave our bags in the room and go for a walk."

Justin peered at Yedley. "Is that really what you want to do?"

Yedley sighed. "No. What I want to do is to bury myself under a bunch of blankets and try to forget about my parents. I'm sorry. I know you worked hard to organize this, but I don't think I'm up for much right now. Maybe in a few hours?"

Justin kissed Yedley's hair again. "Whatever you want. These two days are for you. And don't say it's not fair to me. I can think of nothing better than to spend two days buried in bed with you." Justin paused. "Wait. I only booked one room, and I know how what I just said sounded, but I'm not saying we have to share a bed or that we have to do anything."

Yedley chuckled and shook his head. "Don't worry about it. I don't have a problem sharing a bed with you or doing whatever you had in mind."

"I have nothing in mind, I promise." But Justin could see that Yedley was teasing him, and he felt better. He probably should have booked two bedrooms, but he'd thought Yedley would probably either need to go home or need comfort. And yes, he hoped something more might happen between them. He'd been keeping his distance because he knew Yedley was still getting used to living in Gillham and having his brother in his life again, but maybe he should push at least a little. He'd back off immediately if Yedley wasn't ready, of course, but Yedley couldn't know how important he already was Justin if Justin didn't tell him.

"That's a pity, because I certainly had something in mind when I agreed to spend today and tomorrow with you."

Maybe Yedley was ready for more after all.

They only had one night, and Justin wanted to make the most of it while making sure Yedley was comfortable. "Since you're not up for a walk on the beach, we can go to bed."

Yedley's smile widened. "I'm more than okay with that."

Justin hadn't expected it, but he was on board. The only reason he'd been planning to take things slow was that he thought that was what Yedley needed. But Yedley seemed sure of himself, and Justin wouldn't treat him like a child. Yedley was an adult, and he knew his own mind. If he thought he was ready for this, Justin would believe him.

Whatever *this* was.

Justin checked in once they were inside. The place was cute, but he only had eyes for Yedley. He wasn't even embarrassed by the fact that he and Yedley were obviously going to spend the rest of the day in the room. He doubted it was the first time the lady who did the check-in had seen this, but thankfully she didn't say anything.

He'd had relationships, and he'd wanted men in his bed, but none of them as much as he wanted Yedley. The bond between them thrummed with anticipation and pleasure, even though Justin didn't know what was about to happen.

He was sure the room was cute and comfortable, but he couldn't look away from the bed as soon as they stepped in. He forced himself to lock the door behind them and dropped both their bags down by the wall.

When he turned toward the bed again, Yedley was spread onto it. He was still dressed, but it was enough to make Justin's cock twitch in his jeans. He swallowed and forced himself to talk slowly. "What did you have in mind? Do you want me to turn the TV on? We can cuddle under the blankets and talk about what happened."

Yedley sat up. "I don't want to talk. I've talked enough for today, especially about this situation. I don't even want to think about it again."

"What do you want, then?"

"I want you to join me on the bed. Possibly naked, but I can take care of that bit for you."

Justin blinked. He *definitely* hadn't been expecting that. "You want to have sex with me?"

"Who wouldn't? You're hot, but more importantly, you're my mate. I know I've been keeping some distance between us, but it's not because I don't want you or because I don't feel the bond. I do. I just had some things to figure out before I allowed myself to focus on you."

"And did you figure them out?"

"I'm starting to. Talking to my parents was a big part of that, and now that's over, and I feel free. I'm sad, but I still feel better than I did yesterday. And I don't just want to have sex with you. I want to bond with you."

Justin opened his mouth, but he had no idea what to say.

"I know it's sudden," Yedley continued. "And of course, you can say no. It would probably be better if you did, because we haven't known each other long and we might be making a mistake, but we're mates. It's important to me, and I hope it's important to you, too. I realize being mates isn't everything and that we might still fight and have problems and everything, but I want this."

"Why?" Justin realized how harsh that sounded. "I'm not saying no, but I need you to be honest with me. Why do you want to bond with me?"

"I want something in my life. Something that's mine. Something that's good, after everything."

"I'm already yours."

"Exactly. And I want that to be official."

That was more than good enough for Justin.

He didn't want Yedley to change his mind, and while he doubted that would happen, he wasn't about to waste time. He quickly stripped, forcing himself not to think about the fact that this was the first time Yedley saw him naked. From Yedley's expression, he seemed to enjoy what he was seeing.

"Wait," Yedley said.

Justin froze before stepping out of his jeans. "What?" Had he changed his mind?

"Do you have anything? Lube?"

Dammit. "No." Justin hadn't expected them to have sex today.

Yedley's expression fell. "Okay." He brightened. "We can work around that. Just get over here."

Justin obeyed. He crawled on top of Yedley and looked down at him. Yedley had gotten naked while Justin stripped, and his skin was warm and silky against Justin's. "You do know that sex isn't necessary to bond, right?" he asked.

Yedley rolled his eyes. "Of course I do." He wrapped himself around Justin, and Justin realized it wouldn't take long for him to come. There might not be any kind of penetration involved today, but it didn't matter. Sex was sex, however it happened. He was more than happy to rub against Yedley until they both came. Besides, he knew enough about bonding to understand they'd both come faster than they expected. Not only were emotions involved, but the bond was, too, and being able to feel what Yedley was feeling would feed into Justin's pleasure, and vice versa.

Yedley pressed a hand against Justin's heart, and Justin knew what was about to happen. He'd thought they'd have more time, but if this was how Yedley needed things to go, he was willing to follow his mate's lead.

He pressed his palm against Yedley's hand, startling Yedley. Yedley looked at him with wide eyes, and Justin nodded. "You want to do it before we do anything?"

"I want to do it *while* we're doing it." Yedley snickered, and Justin was grateful that his mate wasn't thinking about his parents right now. He was happy he could do this for Yedley, even though it didn't feel like enough.

But he shouldn't be thinking about Yedley's parents, either.

Yedley hooked his feet around Justin's thighs. He rubbed one up and down Justin's leg, making Justin shiver in pleasure.

"You know this is going to be fast once we start bonding, right?" Justin asked.

"I expect it to. I talked to my brother."

"Please tell me he didn't go into details." Justin didn't want to think about Pryderi having sex and bonding with Nate. Actually, he didn't want to think about Pryderi at all right now.

Yedley shook his head. "He told me that everything is heightened when you bond, so I expect both of us to come quickly. It's not a deal-breaker." He surged up to kiss Justin, and Justin finally let go.

If this was what Yedley wanted, it was what Yedley would get.

Justin was right there with him anyway. He'd wanted to bond with Yedley since the moment he'd realized they were mates, and he'd thought he'd have to wait much longer for that to happen. He was glad he wouldn't. He wanted them to start this together, to explore what the future held for them. This was a new start for Yedley, and Justin wanted to be part of it.

Justin continued kissing his mate and started moving his hips while Yedley's hand heated. It was too warm, almost to the point of pain, but it was easy to forget about it with the pleasure already building in Justin's groin.

"You too," Yedley said. He tilted his head to the side, and Justin knew what he wanted.

Yedley didn't need to say it. Justin's instincts were riding him hard, and he'd been fighting against them not to bite Yedley. Now that he had the authorization to do it, he wasn't going to back down.

His fangs were already out, and the side of Yedley's neck offered to him made something twist in his stomach. He struck, sinking his teeth into Yedley's neck. The taste of Yedley's blood exploded on Justin's tongue, and Justin drank it down while the pain in his chest reached a peak.

Then it disappeared. Everything did except Yedley and the bond stretching and snapping between them, finally complete. Justin could feel Yedley's pleasure, tinted with a hint of sadness and pain. Justin ignored those because there was nothing he could do about them, and instead, he pushed a hand between them and awkwardly wrapped it around both their cocks.

He probably wouldn't have needed to do that. Yedley thrust harder against him, using his legs to push himself up. Justin slid his teeth out of Yedley's neck so he wouldn't hurt him more than had already been necessary, and he quickly licked the wound. Yedley's taste in his mouth, his presence in his arms, Justin's hand on both their cocks, all of that was overwhelming. Justin screwed his eyes shut and pressed himself harder against Yedley until it was almost impossible for him to move.

Yedley came first. His back arched under Justin, and Justin did his best to wait until Yedley slumped, his orgasm over, to come. He wanted to take care of his mate, and right now, this was the best way he could do it. Yedley's pleasure still lingered as Justin let go of his cock and took himself in hand. He pulled on his dick, Yedley still wrapped around him as if he never wanted to let go, and that thought made Justin feel warm all over.

He didn't know what loneliness was. He'd never lost his family. But he knew that his future was complete now. He'd never be alone, because Yedley would always be with him.

He had to roll off Yedley once it was over. Justin didn't want to hurt him, and he felt like his body weighed a ton right now. He was only slightly surprised when Yedley rolled with him and snuggled against him, burying his face against his neck. Justin stroked a hand down Yedley's back. They needed to clean up, but it could wait. "How are you feeling?"

"I thought you could feel it," Yedley muttered.

"I can, but I want you to tell me."

Yedley sighed. "I'm okay. I'm a bit sad, but I'll get over it."

That was all that mattered to Justin. He wanted Yedley to be happy, and he'd do everything he could to me that happen.

CHAPTER FOUR

The job hadn't become less boring while Justin and Yedley had been away. Justin hadn't expected it to, and to be honest, he didn't mind. He had a hard time focusing, because all his thoughts were on Yedley rather than on what he was doing. He knew it was stupid, because he'd get hurt if someone was squatting in the buildings he and his new team were exploring, but he couldn't focus. Now he knew how Pryderi had felt when he realized Nate was his mate. It made sense that he didn't want to be an enforcer anymore.

Justin would quit, too, if he could. He realized it was only because he wanted to spend more time with Yedley, and that the feeling would probably fade eventually, once they both got back to normal life. But *what* was normal life for them?

Yedley was still dealing with a lot. He might have gotten the conversation with his parents out of the way, but that didn't mean he was over it. No matter how hard he tried to convince Justin that he was okay, and no matter that he'd expected his parents to react the way they had, the reality of it had to hurt. Justin couldn't even imagine what Yedley was going through, and he wasn't surprised that Yedley had been isolating himself again. Not physically, but mentally. Justin could feel what Yedley felt, which was the main reason he hadn't pushed. Yedley wanted to be with him, but he understandably needed time.

"Another warehouse?" someone groaned.

Justin blinked. He'd been so deep in his thoughts that he hadn't realized Nadha had shimmered him and the others to their next building. "I don't understand how such a small town as Gillham has so many warehouses." At least this one was on the smaller side.

Lorcan shook his head. "I didn't know it had so many. You're right, it doesn't make sense."

"It does if you think that Gillham became what it is now only in the past twenty or so years," Sue answered, walking past them on our way to the warehouse. "It's a cute little town now, but it wasn't always like this."

Justin wasn't up for a history lesson, so he kept his mouth shut even though he wanted to ask what Gillham was twenty years ago, and he followed Sue toward the entrance.

This warehouse didn't even have a door anymore. It had fallen a while ago from the looks of it, and what was left was what looked like a dark mouth ready to swallow them.

Justin had always been too dramatic.

"I hate this job," Davis muttered as they walked into the abandoned building.

It stank. There was no other word for it. It was as if something big had decided to die in there, which Justin could imagine was several dozens of rats. He doubted anything bigger had come close to the town with all the shifters living here, although he might be wrong. As Sue said, the town was nothing like it had been when this warehouse was built and had later been abandoned.

"Me too," Lorcan agreed.

Justin rolled his eyes. This wasn't the best part of the job, that much was true, but it wasn't as bad as some of the things Justin had seen—and smelled. Not one of the best things, either, but they were adults, and this *was* their job.

"We haven't seen Yedley around a lot yet," Lorcan said, startling Justin.

Justin frowned at him. "We were talking about how much you hate your job. What does Yedley have to do with that?"

Lorcan shrugged. "Just trying to make conversation and to distract myself from this place."

"I see." They needed to focus on the job, but Justin doubted anyone had stayed in this warehouse in at least ten years. The Beasts might have low standards, but even they wouldn't have been able to live here.

It wasn't just the smell. There hadn't been a door up in at least a few years, and most of the windows were shattered. That meant that water, animals, and whatnot had come in. There was mold and moisture on the floor and walls. For some reason, the floor was sticky, and Justin didn't want to think about why. And of course, there was no light. They'd come during the day, but even the sun outside wasn't enough to illuminate the entire main room of the warehouse.

"Be careful on those stairs," Sue yelled.

Justin wasn't about to go near them. Nadha could grab a few of them and shimmer to the upper floor if it was needed, but again, Justin didn't think anyone had climbed the stairs in at least a decade. They were concrete, but they were crumbled, and they didn't look like they'd hold a rat's weight, let alone a human adult.

"So? What's up with Yedley? Are you two not getting along?"

"How do you even know about him?" Justin asked. He'd been trying to make friends with the team, but it wasn't like he'd told them all his darkest secrets. Not that Yedley was a dark secret, but still. Justin understood how unstable Yedley felt right now, and since he wouldn't force him into something he might not want, he'd been careful about who he told about what they were to each other.

He hadn't even told Pryderi they'd bonded yet. He didn't mind waiting, not when the reward would be having Yedley in his life.

Lorcan snorted. "Everyone knows about him. We know

he's the main reason you asked to be transferred here. I mean, it makes sense. You're always at the bar, and we all know it's not for your blond friend."

"Pryderi."

"Yes, him. His mate is Nate."

"They're not the only ones who are in the bar a lot. I could be going to meet with someone else." Besides, Justin might spend a lot of time at the bar, but not with Yedley.

"Well, Nate is out as well, and I don't think you're interested in one of the customers. There is Nate's brother, of course, but we've all seen you with the blond cutie."

Justin was tempted to ask when and where, but he wasn't sure he wanted to know the details. "Yes, I transferred here because of Yedley."

"He's your mate, right?" Davis asked. He poked at something on the ground with the boot and jerked back when the thing moved. A rat that was bigger than most cats skittered away from the pile of debris—whatever it had been. Davis grimaced and looked like he might make a run from the door.

"He is." Denying it would be useless, and Justin didn't want to do it. He might not be sure where he and Yedley stood, but there were bonded. They were in this for the rest of their lives.

They had time to work things out, which was the main reason Justin hadn't pushed. He wanted to do more, but he didn't know how or what. Yedley was dealing with the loss of his parents, which was made worse by the fact that his parents had deliberately abandoned him. He had to get used to a new life—a new town, a new job at the bar, a new way of life. Living in Gillham was nothing like living with the tribe. Yedley was freer than he'd been with the tribe, but being part of the pack also came with constrictions and conditions.

And of course, he had to learn how to live with Justin in his life.

"I don't get it," Lorcan said. "If you're mates, how come you're not spending more time together? I understand taking things slow, but this looks like it's too slow."

"It's not." And Justin wasn't sure he was comfortable talking this out with Lorcan and Davis.

They were good guys, and they were his team members. That meant he'd spend a lot of time with them in the next few years unless one of them quit being an enforcer or asked to be transferred. It was possible, but most enforcers tended to stay in one place for years. It helped to keep the teams together. So Davis and Lorcan would be a big part of Justin's life in the future, along with the rest of the team. He wanted to feel like they were a family like his old team had been, but that would take time.

But one of them had to take the first step, and Lorcan and Davis were reaching out. Maybe Justin could reach back.

It was overwhelming. It wasn't the first time Yedley had tried to work at the bar, but his brother usually made sure he did so when there weren't too many people there. Today, though, it looked like half the town had decided to have lunch at Nate's bar, and Yedley wasn't sure how to deal with it.

But he had to. He'd told Pryderi and Nate he wanted to do this, even though it wasn't true. He *had* to do it, though. He needed to find a way to give back everything Nate and Pryderi had given him. They hadn't put conditions on him living in one of their guest rooms, but not doing anything didn't feel right. Besides, it gave Yedley a chance to stop thinking about his parents.

He'd loved having two days, or a day and a half as it was, to focus on Justin. He wanted more time, but as soon as they'd come back to Gillham, it was as if thoughts of his parents and what had happened with them had taken over Yedley's brain, and he couldn't stop thinking about it.

So here he was, behind the bar washing glasses and trying to stay away from the customers filling the bar. He wasn't good enough to be a waiter yet, and he didn't think he'd ever be. He had no idea when he wanted to do with his life, but as much as he loved Pryderi and liked Nate, he wasn't sure working at the bar was something he wanted to do long term. As it was, though, it was a way to distract himself.

Or at least, it should be, but not having to deal with the customers meant that Yedley had more than enough time to think about his parents. Washing glasses wasn't as distracting as he'd hoped it would be.

Yedley sighed. He'd known how things would go. He'd known his parents wouldn't accept him and that they'd kick him out just like they'd done with Pryderi. He hadn't hoped for anything different.

So why was he so distraught over this? He shouldn't be. He'd expected it. But it still hurt, much more than what he'd been through when he'd been kidnapped. The only way to make it stop was to give himself time, but Yedley felt like he didn't have any. He wanted to start living. He wanted to leave his past behind and focus on his future with Justin. They were bonded, yet they barely talked to each other, and Yedley knew it was his fault. Justin was an angel, giving him time and space, but Yedley didn't *want* time and space. He wanted Justin, and the only reason he didn't have him was himself.

Yet for some reason, he couldn't bring himself to contact Justin. They saw each other regularly. Justin came to the bar almost every day, and they talked, but never about what they were doing as a couple. Yedley wasn't even sure they *were* a couple. They'd bonded, and they'd had sex, but when he looked at Nate and Pryderi, he could see their relationship was nothing like what existed between him and Justin.

The door opened, and Yedley was grateful to have

something else to focus on. He wouldn't be the one to serve whoever was walking in, but for a few seconds, his brain had something else to think over.

When he saw who had walked in, he wished he hadn't looked.

His hands shook as he put down the glass he was holding before he could drop and break it. He swallowed, his mouth suddenly dry, and looked up again.

The man was still there. Yedley didn't know his name, but he'd never forget the first and only time he'd seen him.

Yedley been in a cage. He'd been kidnapped a few days before, and he was terrified. The van he'd been moved in had just arrived at the empty building where the Beasts had kept him and the others. One of the Beasts had reached into the cage to transfer him, but someone had come in, and he'd pushed Yedley back in. He'd covered the cage, but not well, and Yedley had been able to peek out.

The man who'd walked into the bar had brought something to the Beasts. Yedley had no idea what it was or what the man's name was, and he never wanted to find out.

"Everything okay?" Nate asked.

Yedley leaned closer to his brother-in-law, keeping his focus on the man. One of the waitresses led him to a table, and Yedley breathed easier when the man sat with his back to him. "I need to call someone." Yedley had no idea who he was supposed to call in this case, though.

Justin was an enforcer. He'd know.

"That man," Yedley continued.

Nate looked around. "The one who came in just now?"

"Yes. He was with the Beasts. I don't know if he was a gang member or if he was just doing business with them, but I'm sure I saw him there."

Nate's expression hardened. "Stay here. Unless you think he'll recognize you?"

"I doubt that. He never saw me, and he didn't stay long."

"Okay. Stay here and try to act normally. I'll go to the backroom to grab a few bottles of something, and I'll make a phone call." He squeezed Yedley's forearm. "You're safe here. Even if he does recognize you and tries to hurt you, no one here will allow him to come anywhere near you. I promise."

Yedley knew Nate was right. The bar was full, and a lot of the people there were friends of Nate's or regulars. Most of them wouldn't hesitate to step in if something happened. Yedley might not be friends with them himself, but they'd seen him often enough to be aware of who he was.

Still, Yedley felt like he couldn't breathe the entire time Nate was away. He kept looking at the man, but the man never noticed him. He'd ordered a burger, and he was focused on his food. Nate had been gone for far longer than Yedley thought he would be, and the bar door opened before he got back.

Yedley took a step toward the hallway to leave, but he relaxed when he saw who was stepping in.

Nate had done it. He'd called the enforcers, and they'd arrived.

"Stay out of it," Nate said as he slid behind the bar next Yedley. "They want to talk to you later, but they're going to take care of him first."

That was more than okay with Yedley.

Then Justin stepped in.

Yedley hadn't realized that this was his new team, and he wasn't sure what to do. Justin barely looked at him. His attention was focused on the man Nate pointed out for them. Yedley had been frightened for himself, but now he was terrified for Justin. What if the man tried to attack him? What if he hurt Justin?

But this was Justin's job. Even when Yedley couldn't see him, this was what Justin did. It was worse now because it was in front of Yedley's eyes, and Yedley didn't want to see this go down. He didn't want anything to happen to Justin, and that made him realize how important Justin was to him. He already knew it, since Justin was his mate and they'd bonded, but he hadn't allowed himself time to think it over. It had been safer—it had *felt* safer—to keep Justin at arm's length.

But not anymore. The possibility of losing Justin was terrifying, and it made Yedley realize that he was wasting precious time. He and Justin were in this for the long haul, but anything could happen. They could lose each other, and what would Yedley have left? Memories? He had so few of them with Justin, but he wanted more.

Yedley shouldn't have worried. There wasn't enough space for the entire team to crowd the man at the table, and only three team members were there, including the Nix. She shimmered the man away before he could make a scene, and barely anyone in the bar even noticed it. Yedley blinked at the space that was now empty, unsure how to feel about it.

"Okay?" Nate asked.

Yedley nodded. "Yes. Thank you."

Nate patted Yedley's shoulder and went back to work. Yedley was unsettled, but he thought it was the best thing he could do, too.

Until Justin stepped up to the bar.

Yedley should have expected it. Justin would want to make sure he was okay, even though he could feel what Yedley felt. Yedley didn't know what to do with this. He wanted to tell Justin he was okay. He wanted to grab his hand and drag him up to his bedroom. He wanted to bury himself in Justin, to forget everything else in the world for a few hours.

So of course, he barely glanced at his mate when Justin moved closer.

Yedley couldn't seem to be able to look Justin in the eye. That was fine with Justin. As long as Yedley was okay, he could relax. "You're okay?" he asked.

Yedley stared at the glasses on the counter and nodded. "I am."

"Nate told us what happened, but I'd like to ask you a few questions if you feel up to answering them."

"There's nothing much to say. I remembered the man you took away from when I was kidnapped. I was kept in a cage. When the Beasts finally got me into the building where Calvin was, they started moving me to a new cage, but someone came in, and one of them covered the old one. They didn't cover it well enough, though, and I managed to see the man. He was there to give something to the Beasts, and that's all I know. I have no idea what he was handing over, what his name is, or anything else. But I thought you should know about him."

"You did well. I'll let Sue know, but I don't think she'll have more questions for you since you know so little. Do you want me to stay?"

Yedley shook his head. "I'm working. So are you. We should probably go back to what we're supposed to do."

"We will. I just wanted to make sure you were fine. I'll come back later tonight, and we can talk a bit more, if that's okay with you."

Yedley nodded, his blond hair shifting with his movements. Justin wanted to bury his hands into it, but he knew better than to touch Yedley without making it abundantly obvious he was about to do that.

"I'll see you tonight, then," Justin said before moving away.

He went back to the team. They would have to file paperwork, and he hated paperwork.

He quickly talked to Sue, and as he'd thought, she didn't have any more questions for Yedley. She knew where to find him if she did, though, so the team headed out, minus Nadha, Rose, and Janelle, who were at the council jail to interrogate the man they'd just arrested.

"That was weird," Davis said.

"I don't think it was. Honestly, I'm not surprised some people in town were working with the Beasts." They didn't need to be part of the gang to work with them.

"That's not what I meant. When we got the call, I thought you'd be frantic over your mate. I didn't think you'd head out with us. Don't you want to stay with him and make sure is okay?"

"I already know he is."

"Maybe, but don't you want to hang around for a bit? Make sure nothing else happens?"

Justin shook his head. He could feel Yedley in the back of his mind, with his worry and the lingering of fear, but also the warmness of affection. Yedley knew Justin care for him, and he didn't need Justin to hover around him. "He's safe. Nate will make sure of that."

"You don't even look worried."

"I was, but I'm not anymore. I can feel what he really feels. I'll know if something happens."

"Still. Aren't you worried? No offense, but the two of you don't exactly look like a loving couple. Don't you, like, regret bonding with him?"

"Of course not," Justin snapped. He cleared his throat. He knew Davis meant well, even though he didn't appreciate having his teammate stick his nose into his business. "I'll never regret bonding with Yedley. He has hang-ups, just like everyone else, and he works things out better on his own. I don't want to crowd him."

"But he's your mate. Isn't that kind of the point?"

Justin shook his head. "We have time. Even if he needs years to work things out, I'm okay with it. I know things will eventually work out."

Justin was grateful when Davis finally let it go. He didn't want to talk about it anymore, because there was nothing to say.

He didn't regret bonding with Yedley or giving Yedley time. He might not have been through the same things as Yedley, but he could understand why Yedley needed to work things out on his own. When Yedley was ready, he'd reach out to Justin. In the meantime, Justin would hang around and make sure Yedley knew he was there for him, whatever he needed.

Just like Justin had expected, paperwork was boring. There wasn't much to write, since Nadha, Rose, and Janelle were taking care of the interrogation. They didn't need the rest of the team to join them, which meant Justin and the others were stuck in pack territory. They couldn't continue going through the abandoned buildings without the entire team being there, especially Nadha.

Since they didn't have anything to do, Justin left the team in the living room of the enforcers' building and went to his bedroom. He could take a nap or maybe work on unpacking more of his stuff. Although he supposed he should probably not do that since he wasn't planning on staying in the enforcers' building for long. He wanted a home. This was the last time he planned to move. He wouldn't leave Gillham, not unless Yedley wanted to, and that wouldn't happen. Yedley was in Gillham to stay, to be with his brother, and to build a new life.

Justin hoped they'd eventually live together, and that meant he wanted to find the perfect house. That was why he hadn't rushed and why he'd moved into the enforcers' building rather than looking at houses to buy.

He took off his boots and dropped onto the mattress. The bed was tiny, but he was used to it, since he'd lived in the enforcers' wings in Whitedell, too.

Moving to Gillham had been a spur of the moment decision, but he wasn't regretting it, and he didn't think he would. In a way, it was similar to living in Whitedell, and that was reassuring. But there was a lot of hope and opportunities, and Justin was grateful he had them. He didn't have to rush into making any decision.

Justin?

Justin jerked at the sound of Yedley's voice in his mind. He'd known they could do this, but it was the first time Yedley reached out to him in their minds. He hadn't wanted to overstep, so he hadn't tried, either. *Yedley? Is everything okay?*

Yes, don't worry. I just wanted to talk, I guess.

Justin settled back against the bed, making himself comfortable. He didn't know how long Yedley would want to talk, and he hoped Sue wouldn't need him. Justin wanted to give Yedley all the attention he deserved. *Of course.*

There was a pause before Yedley said, *I'm sorry I've been distant. I never meant to hurt you.*

I'm fine. Don't worry about that.

But it's not okay. You shouldn't have to deal with this. I wanted us to bond, and we did, but now I can't seem to allow myself to get close to you.

Justin sighed. *I expected this to be hard, Yedley. I know you've been through a lot, and that's why I've been giving you space.*

But you shouldn't have to give me space. We're bonded.

And that means we have all the time in the world to make things work. Don't obsess over this, Yedley. I want you to be happy, and if that means leaving you alone for a while to figure things out, I don't mind doing it.

What do you want?

That was a heavy question. Justin wanted to answer

honestly, but he was afraid he would push Yedley to do something he wasn't ready for. *I want to be with you, of course. I wouldn't have agreed to bond with you otherwise.*

And I'm not giving you what you want.

Not yet, but that's okay. I told you I understand, and I do. You'll be ready when you're ready, and I don't want to freak you out or push you away by asking too much of you too soon. You have time, Yedley. I promise.

Maybe I don't want time. Maybe I want to be with you, too.

Justin chuckled. *Maybe?*

Okay. I do want to be with you. That's one thing I'm sure of. I'm just, I don't know. I feel awkward, like I'm not myself. I'm afraid to do the wrong thing.

You don't have to do anything different. Talk to me. That's the only way we'll get to know each other. And the only way they'd fall in love.

And Justin wanted that. He wanted forever with Yedley.

Yedley had no clue what he was doing, but he liked it. It was easier to talk to Justin when Justin wasn't in front of him, even though Yedley still felt awkward.

Talking is good, he said.

It is.

Where are you now?

Yedley felt Justin's flash of amusement.

In bed.

Oh God. I swear I wasn't trying to start something. I didn't expect you to be in bed. It was just after lunch. What was Justin doing in bed?

I realize that. I'm going to go downstairs in a bit to have lunch, but since a few of the team members took that guy to the council jail and are interrogating him, the team can't move. I thought I could take a nap before lunch.

So I'm disturbing you.

Never. Justin's sounded so convinced of that that Yedley believed him.

Yedley still wasn't sure why he had contacted Justin this way, but he was glad he had. He wanted to get to know Justin because they were starting a life together, even though Yedley had kept his distance. That wasn't going to last forever. He'd make sure of it. And until he finally felt comfortable enough to reach out to Justin and be his mate the way he ought to be, he wanted them to be at least friends.

He wanted so much more than that, though. He wanted to be in love with Justin. He wanted Justin to be in love with him, which he realized wouldn't happen if he didn't let Justin in. The thought was terrifying. Yedley was afraid Justin would hurt him the way his parents had, but he needed to stop thinking that.

Justin wouldn't, just like Pryderi wouldn't. Yedley could trust them. Now, if only his heart would follow his brain, things would be peachy.

"Yedley?" Nate asked from the hallway.

Yedley had snuck into the break room to talk to Justin, but it looked like it was time to go back to work. "Yes?"

"You can go home if you want, but I'd be grateful if you came back to work."

"I'll be right back."

"Good." Nate chuckled. "Because there are a lot of glasses to wash."

He was teasing Yedley, and it was something Yedley wasn't used to. Yedley realized he wasn't doing a lot for Nate by washing dirty glasses, but right now, it was the only thing he felt ready for, and Nate hadn't asked more of him.

Yedley turned his attention back to Justin. *I need to go. People are starting to leave after the lunch rush, and I need to get started on the dirty glasses.*

Doesn't Nate have a dishwasher?

Yedley couldn't help it—he laughed. *Of course he does. But there's nothing else I can do in the bar right now, and I need to repay him for the fact that he's letting me live in one of his guest rooms.*

Somehow, I doubt he thinks that.

Yedley knew Nate didn't. He and Pryderi had told both him and Calvin that they didn't need to do anything to repay them. They were a family, and Nate's apartment was their home. It was still hard to believe, but Yedley knew it was true.

I'll see you tonight?

If you want to, sure. I'll come to the bar after my shift.

I'll be here.

Yedley went back to work feeling lighter than he had before, which shouldn't have been possible after he'd seen that man in the bar. It was easier for him to get through his work, but he was still relieved when Nate sent him upstairs to take a break. He wanted to check in on Calvin, so he grabbed two sandwiches from the cook who worked at the bar kitchen and went to knock on Calvin's door.

As far as Yedley knew, Calvin hadn't yet left the apartment. Yedley hadn't pushed, and he wouldn't start now. He could see Calvin was getting better even if he didn't leave the apartment. No one expected him to do anything he wasn't comfortable with this soon, not after what he'd been through.

"Calvin? Can I come in?" Yedley called out.

"Of course you can. Why are you even asking?"

Yedley opened the door and snuck in, closing it behind himself. The fact that Calvin trusted him as much as he did always amazed him. They hadn't known each other long, but Calvin had latched on to him when they'd both been prisoners, and Yedley had been grateful for the company and glad he could help Calvin in this small way. He wished he could do more, but at least he could do something. "I brought you lunch," Yedley said, raising the bag the cook had put the sandwiches in.

Calvin smiled. He was still too thin, but he looked better than when he and Yedley had escaped. He was out of fear, at least physically. Yedley wasn't sure how he was mentally, but maybe it was time to push gently. Calvin would never get better if he didn't face his fears.

Of course, Yedley should probably do the same.

Yedley flopped onto Calvin's bed and held out the bag. "Pick whichever you want. I'll eat the other." He was hungry enough not to care what he ate.

"So, what happened earlier? I heard a ruckus, and I'm curious," Calvin said as he sat next to Yedley on the bed.

Yedley looked at him and narrowed his eyes. Calvin liked to hear him talk about what happened outside the apartment, but Yedley was starting to suspect it was a way for him to be part of the world without actually stepping in it. "You could have come downstairs to see."

Calvin shook his head. "You know I can't."

Yedley sat up. "I don't. I understand why you're afraid to leave the apartment, but I'm not asking you to take a walk in town. You could come downstairs to the bar, maybe start when it's empty."

Calvin briefly closed his eyes. He looked like he wasn't sleeping much, which could be because of the nightmares both he and Yedley had or because of something else. Yedley had no idea, and he wasn't willing to force Calvin to do anything he wasn't ready for, but he wanted his friend to know he was there for him.

"You know you can talk to me," he said, squeezing Calvin's knee.

"I know."

"Then why aren't you? Nothing you say will scare me away, I promise." Yedley didn't know how to make Calvin see that, but he hoped Calvin was listening.

Calvin looked at him for a long time, and Yedley held his breath. He hoped it meant that Calvin was finally going to open up. They were friends, and they'd been through hell together, but Calvin was very closed off when it came to his personal life. Of course, Yedley wasn't sure of how much of a personal life Calvin had, since he spent all his time in the apartment, but he wouldn't be surprised if Calvin was having trouble dealing with his past. He'd spent years in labs, being hurt and tortured. Yedley was surprised how healthy Calvin still was after that, both physically and mentally.

Calvin sighed and looked away. "You want to know what's going on? All right. But I warn you, you aren't going to like it."

"Tell me, Calvin. I'm not going anywhere."

"I'm not entirely human anymore."

That was *nothing* like what Yedley had expected. "How so?"

"I don't know how they did it, and I don't know why, but they turned me into a bat shifter."

Yedley should have expected that. Well, not the bat shifter bit, but the fact that Calvin wasn't entirely human anymore. He'd been in those labs for years. Of course the scientists had experimented on him. Yedley had no idea what they'd been trying to do, but the result was that Calvin was a shifter now. "And you thought I was going to push away because of that?"

Calvin shrugged. "Maybe not you."

But someone else. Of course. "Nate won't care. He loves you." If there was one thing Yedley was convinced of, it was that. Nate was so obviously over the moon to have his brother back that Yedley suspected he'd accept Calvin even if he could turn into a purple cow.

"I know that. But he loves the old Calvin, the one I was before I was taken. What if his feelings change once he finds out I'm not that Calvin anymore?"

Yedley took Calvin's hand. "He already knows you're not that Calvin anymore. You've been through too much to be the same boy still, and Nate is aware of that. You should give him more credit."

"I just don't want to disappoint him. I want things to be normal, and I don't know how to make that happen."

"I don't think anyone knows how to make that happen."

"You don't understand. I'm a bat shifter, but I wasn't born that way. I have no idea how to control the shift."

Yedley frowned. "I don't understand."

"I shift without meaning to. Why do you think I've been hiding in this room? At least when I'm here, no one can find out about it."

Oh. Again, it wasn't something Yedley had expected. He also couldn't help Calvin with this because he wasn't a shifter. If Calvin wanted someone to teach him control, he would have to come out as a shifter, and Yedley wasn't sure he was ready for that. "We'll find a way. I promise."

Calvin smiled, but he didn't look convinced. "I hope so."

CHAPTER FIVE

"Why did Lorcan have to fall down those stairs?" Davis whined.

Justin would have rolled his eyes, but he could hear the concern in Davis' voice. "It's not like he did it on purpose."

"I know he didn't, but this was already boring with him around. I can't imagine it's going to get better without him."

"I feel I should be offended," Justin said.

Davis' eyes widened. "I didn't mean anything bad."

"I was teasing you."

"Oh. Sorry."

Justin *did* roll his eyes now. He was trying to fit in, but it was obvious Davis and Lorcan were best friends. That was why Davis had taken Lorcan's injury so hard, even though Lorcan was okay. Nadha had healed him, but Sue hadn't wanted him to continue working with them so she'd sent him back to the enforcers' building for the rest of the day. That meant Davis was without his sidekick. "We're almost done," Justin pointed out.

"Lucky us. Although I think this place is even creepier than the warehouses we had to go through."

Justin looked at the house in front of them. He'd been surprised when instead of a warehouse, Sue had taken them to an old house. The place had to have been gorgeous once, but it had also obviously been abandoned some time ago, and now it was a mess. The paint was peeling, the porch was sinking, and Justin was pretty sure the roof was missing at least a few pieces. Most of the windows were broken, but the front door was closed. "Does Sue really think the Beasts use this place?"

Davis shrugged. "I don't know. She's the boss."

Justin agreed with that, but he doubted anyone had lived there in a while. The Beasts might be part of a gang, but even they needed a place where it wouldn't rain on their heads. "I guess we need to go through it, even though it's obvious it's empty."

Davis snorted. "Like I said, Sue's the boss. I do what she tells me to do, even when I think she's wrong."

"Davis, Justin, take the front door," Sue said. "Nadha, you should probably shimmer upstairs. That way no one else will fall down the stairs."

Justin snorted softly and carefully climbed the porch steps. They were cracked, and he could see the grass growing under a few of them.

"I'd be careful if I were you," Davis said from behind Justin.

Justin shook his head. "I won't fall on my ass the way Lorcan did, don't worry."

"You better not. I need someone to keep me company today."

Justin was always careful when he was on the job, but especially so today. One member of the team had already been hurt, and if it happened to someone else, Sue would have to take them home again. That would be two days in which they couldn't work all their hours, and even though the last time Justin had used the time to talk with Yedley, he liked his job. He wanted to do it.

The door creaked when Justin pushed it open. It probably hadn't been locked in years, but it had been damaged by water, and Justin had to push harder than he thought he would.

He heard the team move behind him, but he ignored them. Sue had told all of them what she expected from them, and the sooner they were out of here, the fewer chances there were that someone else would get hurt.

The inside of the house smelled of mold and growing things. It made Justin's nose prickle, but he couldn't help but be in awe of the house. It was in bad shape, and Justin had no idea if it could ever be brought back to its splendor, but he wanted to try. It was probably a ridiculous idea. It was a miracle the house was still standing, but it was so easy for Justin to imagine him and Yedley living there. They could keep the original woodwork, give the walls a coat of paint, make this a home for both of them.

Justin had no idea where he'd find the money to renovate this place, but it was worth a try, as long as Yedley was okay with it. Justin wasn't going anywhere without his mate, so Yedley *had* to be okay with it.

"Oh my God, did something die in here?" Davis asked.

Justin ignored his words and pointed to their right. "You go there. I'm taking the left."

"Are you sure we should separate? Because I suspect at least one of us is going to be attacked by a ghost."

"Don't be ridiculous." Justin didn't wait for Davis to whine again. He stepped into what had once been the only living room. There wasn't much left of the furniture, which was good, because furniture provided rats a place to nest. The fireplace was big, and the shelves around it had come down a while ago. The floor under Justin's feet creaked with every movement he made, and he hoped he wasn't about to go through it.

Something caught his eye in the corner of the room. Justin frowned and stepped toward it, and once again, something moved. Justin stiffened. He didn't call Davis, even though he probably should have, but he wanted to make sure the thing moving wasn't a rat. He didn't want the team to think he was ridiculous since he hadn't been working with them long.

It wasn't a rat.

Justin shifted instinctively before he could be attacked. His clothes stretched around him, made precisely for this kind of occasion. They were still tight once Justin was in his werewolf form, but he could move easily enough. He faced the man, expecting him to be big and to wear the insignia the Beasts wore, maybe to charge him and try to take him down before he could react.

The man didn't. Instead of attacking, he stayed pressed in the corner, his hair in front of his face, his arms raised to defend himself.

He wasn't a Beast, that much was obvious.

Justin shifted back to his human form, and he was grateful he wasn't naked like he would have been if he'd shifted into an animal. Werewolves were a mix of wolf and human, and while he became bigger when he shifted, he still walked on two legs and had a vaguely human form. He knew he was intimidating, though. He was furry, and his face resembled that of a wolf. The guy in front of him was already terrified, and Justin was positive he wouldn't attack even if he was human.

Justin didn't know how old the man was, but he couldn't be more than twenty-five if even that. He'd been through better days, but right now, he was a mess.

Justin raised his hands so the man wouldn't think he was about to attack and hoped his shift hadn't freaked out the guy too badly. "My name is Justin."

The man watched Justin with wide eyes. His back was pressed against the wall, and Justin suspected that if he got close enough, he'd find that the man smelled like the house — moldy and dirty. The man's hair was a wild tangle, and Justin wasn't sure if it was brown or if it looked that way because it was dirty.

"Do you live here?" Justin asked. The answer was probably

yes, which was surprising.

The man nodded. "I can leave if you need me to," he said in a rush.

Justin didn't know what Sue would want this man to do. He didn't think the man was part of the Beasts. He was a squatter, and he probably didn't have a safer place to go. Not that this place was safe. It was a miracle the man hadn't hurt himself or that he wasn't sick. "You can stay for now," he said. Justin hesitated. "What's your name?" He wanted to have asked so many more questions, but he doubted he'd get answers.

The man shook his head. "I should leave."

"Do you have another place to go?" Because there had to be a reason the man lived here, and it has to be a good one.

"No."

Justin nodded. "That's what I thought. Stay here. I'll be right back." Justin stepped back into the entrance and yelled for Sue. Of course, that got the attention of the entire team, and a few moments later, they were all gathered in the entrance, circling Justin.

"Are you hurt?" Sue asked.

"I'm not. I found a squatter."

Sue's eyes narrowed. "A Beast?"

"I don't think so. I'm pretty sure the guy is human, although he didn't let me get close enough to smell him." And even if he had, Justin probably wouldn't have been able to smell anything but dirt. "He's terrified of something, and he doesn't have another place to go."

Sue shook her head. "We can't allow him to stay here."

"Not for long, of course. But the guy is frightened. I don't know why, but I'd like him to trust me enough to tell me." If he needed to be protected, Justin was more than ready to do that. It was his job, even if no one had ordered him to do it. "Can we allow him to stay here for a few days? I can come around and make sure he has food and a blanket. I don't think dragging him out of here kicking and screaming will help. It's only going to make him distrust us and be afraid of us as well as whatever else is afraid off."

"Kameron isn't going to be happy. He doesn't like having homeless people in town. We can take the man to one of the shelters, and the pack will make sure he has everything he needs, including an apartment."

Justin was aware of the program Kameron and the pack had put in place to help the people who needed it, but he didn't think this guy would accept any help, not yet. "I'll talk to Kameron, but I think we should give this guy a few days. Please. I'll come by myself I'll make sure he's okay."

Sue sighed. "You're just as stubborn as the rest of us, aren't you?"

She was giving in. Justin nodded, grateful she hadn't put up more of a fight. "Thank you. I promise I won't let him get hurt."

"I hope not. From what you're saying, it's obvious he already has been."

"Yedley, can you grab Calvin and come to the kitchen?" Nate yelled from somewhere in the apartment.

Yedley and Calvin looked at each other. "What do you think he wants?" Yedley asked.

Calvin shrugged. "I have no idea. Maybe he wants to apologize again?"

"For what? Because you were taken?"

"I think he's apologized at least a few dozen times about that."

"Didn't you tell him he didn't have to?"

"Of course I did. I don't think he listened to me." Calvin got up from the bed and stretched. "Let's go see what's going on."

Yedley had no idea why Nate wanted to see both him and Calvin, but he supposed they were about to find out. Maybe it had to do with the bar, although since Calvin didn't have anything to do with that, probably not.

Yedley's stomach churned. Nate wasn't about to tell them they had to leave the apartment, was he? Yedley didn't think that was possible or that Pryderi would allow it even if Nate wanted it, but he couldn't help the fear that gripped him. He only had Pryderi, Nate, and Calvin.

Wait. That wasn't true, not anymore. Yedley and Justin might still be trying to understand how to make things work, but Yedley knew Justin wasn't going anywhere.

And neither were Nate and Pryderi. It was stupid to think they could kick him and Calvin out. They'd never do that.

He swallowed and followed Calvin outside. Nate and Pryderi were both sitting at the kitchen table when Yedley and Calvin walked in, their heads close together. Pryderi was hissing something at Nate, obviously displeased with whatever Nate had in mind. That made Yedley frown, but since it was obvious he couldn't guess what was happening and that he was about to find out, he forced himself not to obsess over it.

Everything would be okay. They had to be.

Nate looked up when he heard Calvin and Yedley. He smiled at them, but it was forced. "Why don't you both sit down?"

Yedley and Calvin obeyed. Yedley wasn't surprised when Calvin reached for his hand under the table and squeezed it. Yedley squeezed back and linked their fingers together as they faced whatever was about to happen.

"I'm sure that by now you've heard what's happening with the Beasts," Nate started.

"They left town," Calvin said.

"They did, and Kameron and Bran are making sure of that.

But that's not what I meant. It seems that the man who created the gang has a grudge against Kameron. He wants to take Kameron down, and he won't hesitate for anything. I wouldn't be surprised if the Beasts came back, and I don't want the two of you to be in town if that happens."

Yedley blinked. "I'm not sure what you mean."

"He wants the two of you to move into pack territory," Pryderi said.

That wasn't what Yedley had expected, but maybe he should have. He knew how overprotective Nate was when it came to his brother, and he didn't blame him. Calvin deserved to be protected after everything he'd been through. He *should* be protected.

"What about the two of you?" Calvin asked. "Would you be coming with us?"

Nate shook his head. "We can't. We have to stay at the bar. But it will be safer for both of you to be gone, just in case something happens."

Yedley cringed. He knew the real reason Calvin wasn't leaving his bedroom now, and while he didn't doubt that part of it was fear, he also knew Calvin wouldn't let that fear take over. It was hard, but they were both working on overcoming what had been done to them. It was especially hard for Calvin, but even Yedley knew better than to try to order him around.

Nate continued, "Pryderi and I will help you move, of course. I already contacted Kameron—"

"No." It was a single word, but Yedley could hear the conviction in Calvin's voice.

Nate blinked. "I'm sorry?"

"I'm not leaving. You can't force me."

"I only want you to be safe."

"I understand that. I don't blame you for it, but I'm not leaving."

Nate raked a hand through his hair. "But why? I understand you want to stay near me, but I promise I'll visit every day."

"It's not just that. I'm finally not a prisoner. I don't ever want to go through that again."

"You wouldn't be a prisoner. Besides, it's not like you ever leave your bedroom. It wouldn't change anything."

Calvin got up, the chair dragging on the floor. "Are you blaming me for the way I'm behaving?"

"Of course not. You were gone for years, and you've been through so much that I can't even imagine how you're feeling right now. That's why I want you to be safe."

Calvin shook his head, grabbed Yedley's hand again, and pulled him out of his chair.

Yedley followed. He'd follow Calvin anywhere, even though he had no clue what was happening.

"Where are you going?" Nate asked from behind them.

He heard Nate and Pryderi follow them. When it became obvious that Calvin was going to the bar, Yedley shook his hand out of his. "What are you planning?" he asked.

Calvin hesitated before stepping into the bar itself, but he did, and Yedley had never been so proud of him. Still, Calvin was terrified, and Yedley wasn't sure this was a good idea. "Are you sure you want to do this?" he asked.

Calvin chuckled, but it wasn't a happy sound. "I'm not sure of anything right now, but I need to do this. You heard Nate. He thinks he needs to protect me as if I'm a kid. But I'm not. I'm an adult man, and it's time I start acting like it."

"You don't have to start doing anything. We all understand how hard this is for you."

"You're right, it is. But I don't think things are ever going to change if I don't start pushing myself. Not everyone wants to hurt me. I know that."

With that, Calvin strode into the bar and made a beeline for the counter.

It was the middle of the day, so there weren't a lot of people. Lunch had ended a while ago, and it was still early for dinner. Nate always closed around three PM, so in half an hour. Still, there were a few people around, and everyone turned to look at Calvin when they noticed him.

Yedley had never seen Calvin as anything but a friend, but he couldn't deny Calvin was cute, and he suspected that was what a lot of people there thought, too. It would explain the way they kept peeking at him.

Calvin was visibly relieved once he stepped behind the counter. The barman knew better than to come anywhere close to them, but he nodded at Calvin. "What do you need?" he asked.

"To do something. I don't care what it is, as long as you don't expect me to go out there and start taking orders."

"All right. You can start with the dirty glasses."

Yedley snorted. "You know, that was my job until now."

"Well, you're going to have to find something else to do, because it's my job from now on."

Calvin still looked nervous, but he was there, and he was trying. Calvin was doing this not because he wanted to defy Nate, but because he had something to prove, both to himself and his brother. He had to start living again, and this was his first step toward that goal.

A noise behind him made Yedley turn, where he saw. Nate standing, looking sheepish, with Pryderi next to him.

Nate rubbed a hand on the back of his neck and looked at his brother. "I'm not here to tell you what to do. I want to apologize."

Calvin put down the glass he'd already grabbed. "Pryderi got to you?"

Nate chuckled. "He did. I realize how what I said sounded now. I wasn't trying to order you around, I promise. I'm just trying to keep you safe. I'm terrified something else is going to happen to you and that you'll disappear from my life again. I want to do everything I can to prevent that, but Pryderi pointed out how patronizing I sounded. You're thirty-five. You don't need me to keep you safe."

Calvin shook his head. "I do. I'm glad for everything you did, both before and after I was taken. I'm not trying to be ungrateful. But I need to start moving on, and that won't happen if I hide in pack territory. I promise I'll come to you if I need help or if I feel unsafe, but please, let me do this."

Nate nodded. "Of course."

Things were changing, both for Yedley and Calvin. Yedley had no idea what the future would be like for them, but they *had* a future, and that was the only thing that mattered.

Justin wanted to do something for the man in the house, but he wasn't sure what. He'd promised Sue he'd help, though, and the best way to do that right now was probably to feed the man and try to make him as comfortable as possible. It wouldn't be an easy task if the man insisted he wanted to stay in the house, but Justin could try.

The first step was to buy food. Justin hesitated between going to the grocery store and the bar. The food from the store would stay good longer, even without a fridge to put it in, but it wouldn't be warm. Justin had no clue how long the man had been in the house, but it was obvious it had been a while, and he suspected the man would be glad to have something warm to put in his stomach.

The bar it was, then. Maybe Yedley would be there, and Justin could spend a few minutes with him before leaving. He was looking forward to it after the conversation they'd had through their bond.

Justin was surprised to see Calvin behind the bar when he

stepped in. He blinked, unsure what was happening. Nate was there, too, and he was hovering close by. *That* didn't surprise Justin. Nate had to be going crazy with worry about his brother, yet he was there, supporting him.

Justin's gaze slid to Yedley. He was present, too, but for once, he wasn't behind the bar. That position had been taken by Calvin, and even though it was obvious Yedley was uncomfortable, he was picking up dirty dishes and glasses from the tables and bringing them back to counter, but he stopped when he noticed Justin. He smiled, and Justin walked to his side. "I wasn't expecting to see Calvin here," Justin said.

Yedley shrugged. "Nate tried to get him to move into pack territory. Calvin wasn't happy about it."

Justin chuckled. "I can see that. Is he okay, though?"

"He will be, eventually. It'll take time, but he's working on it, and he has help. What about you? What are you doing here? I thought you'd be at work."

"I was. But Lorcan got hurt, then we found a guy living in one of the empty houses we explored. I'm here to buy him food."

Yedley cocked his head. "You are?"

"Sue wanted me to tell Kameron about the guy, and I will, but I think he's frightened of something, and he needs help. I thought maybe bringing him some food and a blanket or two would make him feel more comfortable with me and that he'll eventually trust me enough that I can move him out of the house. It's in bad shape, and so is he." Justin didn't tell Yedley how much he liked the house and the future he could see for them there, not yet. He wasn't ready.

"So you're here to get food?"

"I know it's early for dinner, but yes. The guy looked like he could use a warm meal."

"I'll talk to Nate and see what we can do. Wait here?"

Justin nodded. "Of course." He sat at the counter while

Yedley disappeared into the kitchen after talking to Nate. Nate tilted his head at Justin, but he barely looked away from his brother. Justin made sure to keep his distance from Calvin, just in case. He'd met Calvin already, of course, but he could tell Nate was on edge, and the last thing he wanted was to freak out either Nate or Calvin.

"Give the cook about twenty minutes," Yedley said as he came back. "He'll have something ready by then."

"That's good. And it gives me time to talk to you."

Yedley hesitated. "I was planning to go with you."

Yedley always managed to surprise Justin, didn't he? "You're welcome to, of course, but this guy is terrified. I don't want him to freak out. I already had a hard time making sure he stayed there now that someone knows that's where he's been living."

"I can stay outside if he's uncomfortable with my presence, but I'd like to go with you."

"Of course." Maybe Yedley would fall in love with the house the way Justin had. It would be a step forward.

"I'll go upstairs and grab a blanket. I'm sure Nate has some spare ones."

Yedley cared. Everyone would have understood if he'd focused on himself and healing from what had happened to him, but that wouldn't be him. He wanted Calvin to get better, and he wanted to help this guy.

Justin had no idea what was in the plastic bag the cook handed to him, but it smelled good. He hoped the man at the house would accept it, but if he didn't, Justin wouldn't mind eating it.

"Ready to go?" Yedley asked. He was carrying a heavy blanket and had bundled himself into a coat. It wasn't that cold outside, but Yedley looked adorable, and Justin knew this was another way for him to shield himself.

"What do you know about this guy, then?" Yedley asked

as they walked to the house.

"Nothing. Not even his name. He wouldn't tell me, and I can't blame him. The entire team was there except for Lorcan, and it had to be scary."

"You need to find out what his name is."

"I'll try. I can't promise anything, though."

"And you said your team leader is allowing you to do this?"

"I'm going to have to talk things out with Kameron, of course, and the house isn't a safe place for this guy to live, but for now, this is the best I could do."

"What about the owners? Are they okay with this guy living in their house?"

Justin had looked into that as soon as he'd gotten back to pack territory. He was curious to know who owned the house and why they'd let it get into the state it was in now. He'd found out that the man who'd owned it had died several years ago. His daughter didn't live in town. She didn't even live in the state. It explained why she'd allowed the house to become the ruin it was now, and Justin hoped that if he reached out to her and offered her to buy the house, she'd agree.

But of course, Yedley needed to be okay with it.

Justin cleared his throat. "The lady it belongs to lives on the other side of the country. I'm planning to contact her and ask her if I can buy the place." Justin probably should have waited to mention that, but Yedley was coming with him, and he wanted to know right away if his mate had the same vision he did of the house and their future.

"Really?"

"It looks bad right now, but I think it would be a great home to live. With you, hopefully."

"You want me to live with you?"

"Eventually. I mean, it's going to take a while to get the house ready. You'll understand when you see it. And of course, I won't buy it if you're against it or if you hate it. But I hope it can be a home for both of us one day, once it's renovated and we're together."

Yedley stopped. "I thought we *were* together."

"I want us to be." But to be a couple, they needed to spend more time together and actually to talk to each other. Of course, they were working on that, but Yedley still looked uncomfortable when he was alone with Justin, and Justin didn't know how to make things better.

"I know it's my fault you're not sure we're together," Yedley said.

"It's not your *fault*. You need time, and I understand that."

Yedley shook his head. "Let's see this house. I'm sure I'll like it." He reached out to Justin, offering his hand.

Even though Justin was surprised, he took it. Their fingers felt good linked together, and while Justin wanted more, this was perfect. It was a step forward for Yedley, and that was more than enough for Justin.

"You weren't kidding when you said it was in bad shape," Yedley said once they reached the house.

Justin already knew that, but seeing it through Yedley's eyes was different. It made him realize just how bad it was. It would take a lot of money to renovate, and Justin didn't know what price the owner would agree to sell for in the first place — if at all.

But they could do this. If Yedley liked it, if he wanted it as much as Justin did, this would be their home.

But first, Justin had to take care of the guy who was already living in it.

The place was a mess. Yedley knew nothing about flipping houses and renovating them except what he'd seen on Nate's

TV, but even he could see that. He had no idea why Justin thought they could do this, that they could transform that shell of a house in a home, but he couldn't deny he could see the charm of the place. Under the peeling paint and rotting wood, it was obvious this house had been beautiful once. He wanted to see it beautiful again.

"What now?" he asked.

"I'm not sure. I think you should stay outside in the beginning, just in case."

"Okay. But yell if you need help." Not that Yedley would be able to do much, but he wouldn't have Justin go in there without backup—even if that back up was him.

He watched Justin disappear inside the house. He'd been surprised when Justin had told him he was planning to buy the place. He'd thought that with the distance between them, Justin might change his mind about moving to Gillham. He was working with one of the enforcers' teams here, but that didn't mean he couldn't transfer back to Whitedell.

Yedley didn't want him to. He wanted a relationship with him, but he had no idea how to make it happen. This was nothing like the relationships he'd had with women. He hadn't cared about them, but he cared about Justin, more than he thought possible. He wanted him and Justin to have a chance at this, and that would only happen if *he* gave them a chance. He would have to find out how to do that, but he was ready to work on it, and work hard.

He could hear Justin moving inside the house, and from the voices, he suspected the man who lived there was in one of the front rooms.

"I brought you something to eat," Justin said.

"Why?" a man asked.

"Because you're hungry. I told you I'd come back."

"I don't understand why."

"There's nothing to understand. Take the bag and eat while

it's warm. And talking about being warm, my mate is out there with a blanket. He won't come in if you don't want him to, but it should help you feel more comfortable in here. This place is freezing, and you shouldn't have to live here."

"I don't want to leave."

"No one is asking you to, I promise. I still have to talk with Kameron, the alpha of the pack in town, but I don't think he'll have a problem with you staying here for a while. He'll be worried, though."

"Why should he be worried?"

"Because no one should live the way you're living right now. I don't know why you're here, and I won't force you to leave. No one will. It would be better for you to find a safer place, though. But that can wait. Right now, I think you should eat and allow my mate to come in to give you the blanket."

Yedley didn't hear if the man gave Justin an answer, but Justin appeared at the front door moments later. He waved Yedley in, and Yedley went. He was careful, because he could see how rough the floor was, and he didn't want to fall on his ass, but Justin was there, telling him where not to walk and holding his arm when he stumbled.

He cared for Yedley. No matter how Yedley felt, how confused and awkward he was, Justin wasn't going anywhere.

"I'm sorry," Yedley told Justin.

Justin frowned. "What are you sorry about?"

"I'm making things difficult for you. I want to have a relationship with you, but I have no idea how to do that. All the people I was with before were women, and they all hoped we'd eventually get married and have children. That's how things work with the tribe. But I was never interested in them, and I knew it from the beginning. This is different. I care for you, and I want things to work between us. I want us to buy this house and make it a home, just like you said. I don't know how to do any of that, but I want it."

Justin smiled and kissed Yedley's cheek. "Stop worrying so much. We both want the same thing, and that's what's important. We'll work everything else out in time."

Yedley nodded. Justin guided him to the left, and Yedley cringed at the state of the house. He couldn't imagine anyone living here. Even the place where he and Calvin had been held hadn't been this bad. They'd been in cages, and it had been cold and funky smelling, but this was even worse.

The man Justin had talked about was in the corner. He was sitting on the floor, his back pressed against the wall. It was obvious he'd been living there a while, and Yedley felt sorry for him. He wanted to help him, but how?

He swallowed and stepped forward. "I'm Yedley, Justin's mate." Yedley knew he looked harmless, and he hoped that would work to his advantage. He held out the blanket. "You can have this. It's not much, but it should help you."

The man hesitated, and he pressed harder against the wall when Yedley moved closer, but he didn't try to run. Yedley gently wrapped the blanket around the man's shoulders. He moved back, but not as far away as he was before, and crouched next to him. "What's your name?" he asked.

The man looked from Yedley to Justin, then down at his burger. "Devon."

"Nice to meet you, Devon."

Devon looked like he wasn't sure what to make of Yedley, and Yedley understood him. He didn't know how to act in this situation, but he wanted to help. He wanted to find a way to make life better for Devon.

"Thank you," Devon murmured.

"You have nothing to thank us for. Anyone would have done this in our place. Can you tell me how you ended up here?"

Devon shook his head, panic filling his eyes. Yedley raised

a hand. "It's okay. You don't have to say anything if you're uncomfortable. We want to help, but we understand you don't trust us yet."

"I can't trust anyone."

"I don't know what you've been through, but I know how you feel. I know promising you can trust me and Justin won't make it happen. Would you say no to having Justin's or my phone number? I'd like for you to be able to reach us if you need help." Except if Devon didn't have a cell phone, he couldn't call. "My brother-in-law owns the bar. It's not far from here, and I'll tell him about you, so he'll know to welcome you if you come by."

Devon shook his head. "You can't tell anyone about me. Please."

If Yedley had to guess, he'd think someone was after Devon. Devon didn't want anyone to know he was there. He was hiding. "I'll only tell him one of my friends might come by, okay? I won't even give him your name if you don't want him to know. But I want you to have a safe place if you ever need one. Please." Yedley wanted to do a lot more for Devon, but if this was all Devon allowed, it would have to do.

But Devon was too young, too fragile to be here. No one deserved to live in a place like this, and Yedley wanted to protect Devon, even though he didn't know him.

Life hadn't been easy for Yedley, but he suspected it had been even worse for Devon. He was young, and he had his entire life in front of him. He shouldn't be spending it like this.

Yedley couldn't do a lot for him if he didn't trust him, but he could work on earning that trust. He could make life a bit more comfortable for Devon, even if Devon stayed here.

CHAPTER SIX

The house was theirs. Well, it was officially Justin's, but since both he and Yedley would live there, Justin considered it theirs, which was why he was on his way to the bar. Of course, that didn't mean much right now. Yedley still lived with his brother, Nate, and Calvin above the bar, and Justin was still stuck in the enforcers' building in pack territory. It would be a while before either of them could move into the house because it was such a mess. But at least now, they could start working on it.

The thoughts made Justin wonder what they were supposed to do with Devon. The man still lived in the house, no matter how many times Justin and Yedley had tried to convince him to move out. He was still afraid, although he'd started getting used to Justin and Yedley, and he'd relaxed with them. They were far from being friends, but Devon was more comfortable, and that meant they'd been able to help him more.

Yedley came every day now. He always brought Devon a warm meal and enough stuff from the grocery store that he'd have something to eat for the rest of the day. Yedley had also brought him toiletries. Devon couldn't shower or anything like that, since there was no running water at the house, but he made good use of the wet wipes Yedley always made sure he had. Justin, on the other hand, had brought Devon new clothes. They were warmer than the ones he'd been wearing when they'd first met, and Justin made sure to wash them and bring them back when he could so Devon always had something clean to wear. Justin was grateful for the washing machines in the enforcers' house, that was for sure.

Justin wanted to continue helping Devon. He wouldn't kick the man out, but he needed to call contractors and have them start working on the house. That meant Devon wouldn't be able to hide there anymore, and Justin had no idea how Devon would take that. He told Devon what he was doing when he'd decided to buy the house, but they hadn't talked about it again yet.

They would have to now.

Justin walked around the bar, not wanting to go in since he was only there to see Yedley. He hadn't told him he was coming by because he wanted it to be a surprise. He knew Yedley might have a problem with what Justin was planning, but this was important for Justin. He prayed Yedley would agree, but he wasn't holding his hopes up.

He climbed the stairs that led to the upper floor. The apartment had two entrances, one that led to the bar, and one that opened on top of this flight of stairs. Justin hoped someone was home, although since Calvin had started working at the bar, everyone was downstairs most of the time.

He knocked. He only had to wait a few moments before the door opened, and Pryderi smiled at him. "Yedley didn't tell me you were meeting him."

"That's because he doesn't know."

"You're surprising him. That's so cute."

Justin rolled his eyes. "I don't mind being cute, and yes, I *am* surprising him, but I don't think it's the way you think."

"Now I'm curious."

"I'm on my way to sign the deed on the house. I want Yedley to come with me so he can sign, too."

"I probably shouldn't be as excited as I am, since it's not my house, and it's a wreck, but I am."

"Me too, although I hope Yedley will sign. You know what

he thinks about him not putting money in the house."

Justin and Yedley had talked about it a few times. Justin hadn't made it a secret that he wanted Yedley to be on the deed, too, but Yedley had refused the few times Justin had mentioned it. He wanted to contribute economically, but he wasn't in a place to do that right now. Justin kept telling him he didn't care, but Yedley had refused so far. Justin had talked to Kameron, though, and he hoped that the deal he was about to offer Yedley was one Yedley would take.

Pryderi grimaced. "He's in his bedroom. You want to come in?"

"Yes, thanks. Don't wait for us. I hope we'll be able to leave in a few minutes, and I'm not sure when we'll be back." He wanted to go visit Devon once this was done to tell him what was happening.

"Good, because Nate is waiting for me downstairs. Calvin is working behind the bar again, and Nate wants me to keep an eye on the customers."

"It's early afternoon. I'm sure the bar isn't that full."

"It's not, but some people make Calvin uncomfortable, and he's already trying so hard. Nate and I are hoping to make this easier for him."

That was one of the reasons Justin was Pryderi's best friend. Pryderi cared, and he always tried to make everyone's life easier—except his own. "I'll call you if anything happens."

Yedley didn't look surprised when he opened his door to find Justin there. Justin arched a brow.

Yedley shook his head and waved him in. "It was either you or Pryderi, and he came around about half an hour ago.".

"I have a surprise for you, and I want you to listen to me before you say anything or make any decision," Justin said. He didn't want them to be late, which meant he had to convince Yedley to come with him as soon as possible.

Yedley blinked, but to Justin's relief, he nodded. "I'm listening."

"I talked to Kameron. We're buying the house, and before you can protest, the pack is giving us most of the money. It's something Kameron always does for his pack members, and even though neither of us has been here long, that's what we are. He wants us to have a good start in Gillham, and I have to admit, this is the best thing I can think of. I know your main reason not to want to be on the deed was that you felt you couldn't contribute economically, but now, neither of us will. We can use the money I put aside to start the renovations, and if you still want to be more involved, you could help with that."

"I'd have no idea where to start."

"Me neither, but it might be fun to find out together." And with the contractors, but that went without saying.

"All right."

Justin took a second to make sure he'd heard that right. "You'll be on the deed? You'll sign?"

"I will. I know how important this is to you, and with the pack stepping in with the money, I don't feel as guilty as I would have if you'd had to get a loan. And I think that helping with the renovation will be a good thing. It will help us put our print on the house and really make it ours." Yedley bit his lower lip. "But what about Devon?"

"Let's go sign all the paperwork. Then we can go to the house and discuss this with him."

Justin felt like he was walking on cloud nine as he and Yedley left the office. They had the keys, even though as they already knew, they didn't need them. They'd been coming and going inside the house for the past several weeks, but now that it was theirs, Justin was planning to put on a real door that could lock.

Of course, he and Yedley had to convince Devon to leave the place, at least until it was renovated. "What would you think about Devon living with us?" Justin asked before he could think better of it. He thought it was a good idea, but he and Yedley were newly bonded. Maybe Yedley would want more privacy.

"I'm so glad you mentioned it. I thought about this a few times, but I wasn't sure you'd be okay with it. It also doesn't solve the problem of where Devon is going to stay while we do the renovations, but I hate the thought of him having to find a new place without help or friends."

"Let's talk to him. I already know he won't agree to this right away, but I wish he didn't live there right now. Maybe we could contact contractors and have them set up the kitchen or something so Devon will be more comfortable." Justin doubted he'd want to leave. For whatever reason, he felt safe at the house, and Justin wanted him to have that. "He could help us renovate as a way to pay rent."

Yedley beamed at Justin. "Thank you."

"What for?"

"For being who you are. For agreeing to this. For wanting to help Devon even though he's been squatting in your house for weeks."

"*Our* house, and as far as I'm concerned, he's a friend and he belongs in the house." Now they only had to make sure Devon was on the same page as they were.

Yedley was relieved. He'd wanted to ask Justin if Devon could continue living at the house for a while, and since he'd refused to sign the deed along with Justin until now, he hadn't felt he had a say in the decision. Now he did, and even better, Justin was on the same page as he was when it came to this.

Yedley wished he could get Devon to leave the house, at

least until it was a decent place to live, but even though Justin thought he might be able to convince him, Yedley doubted it. Devon hadn't talked to either of them about why he was living there, but Yedley knew enough about fear to recognize it when he saw it. Devon was there because he was terrified, and nothing would convince him to leave. That meant Yedley and Justin needed to make the house a safe and comfortable place for him. Now that it was theirs, that was finally possible.

Yedley was looking forward to helping with the renovations. He was used to living rough, so he wouldn't have a problem moving in right now if he could, but he knew neither Justin nor Pryderi would allow that Besides, the tribe might have been similar to the house in that neither had running water or electricity, but at least the tribe members had kept their territory clean. The house was anything but, but now they could change that.

He wanted the house to be his and Justin's. He wanted them to work on it together, even though he had no idea where to start. He was grateful Justin had already thought about the contractors, but Yedley wanted to work alongside them. He realized he couldn't help much, but a little would be better than nothing.

It was weird. Yedley felt like he'd been in limbo ever since he and Calvin had been rescued from the Beasts. He'd had a home in Nate's apartment, and he'd had a family, but it had felt like he was waiting for something to happen, and now, he knew why. This was what he'd been waiting for. Now he had a home and a mate, and he could start *living*.

Of course, he and Justin needed to take care of the house first. Yedley might be used to living rough, but Justin wasn't, and even if he were, Yedley wanted them to start their life together on the right foot.

"Why you think Devon is so scared of leaving the house?" Justin asked.

Yedley would have thought Justin of all people would have realized why. He was an enforcer, and he had to have been through this kind of situation many times. "He's hiding."

"That's what I thought. He's never told you why? Or from whom?"

"He's never even confirmed that's why he's here. He doesn't like to talk about that or about his past, so I didn't push. I was afraid he wouldn't be there the next time I went if I did." And for some reason, Yedley didn't want that to happen.

He supposed that most people would have freaked out at finding a man squatting in their house, but he hadn't. It was obvious Devon needed help, and Yedley wanted to provide that. He didn't know how except by giving him a place to stay and keeping his presence a secret.

But Devon wasn't alone anymore. He had Yedley and Justin, and Yedley hoped that would be enough.

Justin stopped walking and looked around. "We haven't even taken the time to celebrate," he said.

"Celebrate? I don't know what you have in mind, but we can go somewhere later tonight if you want."

Justin grinned and wrapped an arm around Yedley's waist, pulling him against his body. "How about we start right now?"

It was cold, too cold to stand on the sidewalk and make out, but Yedley couldn't find it in himself to push Justin away. He tilted his head toward his mate, smiling when the gesture was enough for Justin to lean down and press their lips together.

"I can't wait until we have our own home. I want to wake up next to you every morning," Justin said.

Yedley loved living with Calvin, Pryderi, and Nate, even though the apartment felt crowded a lot of the time. But like

Justin, he couldn't wait to take the next step in their life.

"I want that, too."

Justin peered at Yedley. "You feel more comfortable with me, don't you?"

Yedley blinked. He did, even though he hadn't realized it until now. He wasn't sure why, except that he and Justin had been spending time together. Maybe now that he knew Justin, it was easier for Yedley to follow his instincts on their relationship and to relax. He was less afraid of making mistakes and sending Justin running. Their relationship wasn't perfect by any means, but it felt more natural than it had in the beginning, and Yedley knew it had a lot to do with the fact that he'd finally relaxed.

He smiled back at Justin. "I do."

"Good. I don't know how long it'll take for the house to be in a good enough shape that we can move in, but I won't wait one second too long to have you in my bed."

Yedley was tempted to tell Justin he could have him in his bed tonight, but even though being with Justin felt more natural now, Yedley knew there was no way he'd be comfortable sharing a bed with his mate while knowing all the other enforcers were in the house. It didn't even have anything to do with them possibly hearing Yedley and Justin having sex. Yedley was still more comfortable with a limited number of people around.

It was kind of ridiculous when he thought about it. He'd been kidnapped, but he hadn't been with the Beasts for long, and they'd never really hurt him. He'd been caged, but what he'd been through was nothing next to what Calvin had survived. He shouldn't have nightmares, and he shouldn't be afraid of people he didn't know. But it was instinct, and he had yet to find a way around it.

But he was happy. He couldn't remember the last time he'd felt this way, and he thought it was because he'd *never* felt this way.

"We should go," Justin said with regret in his voice. "I want to have enough time to tell Devon what's going on and to reassure him that he doesn't have to leave."

They both knew Devon's first thought when they told him they'd bought the house would be to leave. No matter how many times they told him no one knew he was there and that he could stay for as long as he needed to, it was easy to see he didn't quite believe them.

The man was in his usual spot in the living room when they arrived. He'd stopped jumping at every little sound in the house, and he smiled at them when he saw them. He was getting used to their presence, which warmed Yedley's heart. He didn't want Devon to be afraid of him. He didn't want anyone to be scared of him, and even though he knew it wasn't him Devon was terrified of, he felt better seeing the smile on Devon's face.

"We have news," Yedley said.

Devon frowned. "It doesn't sound very good."

"You're wrong. It's really good. Justin and I just bought the house. This place is officially ours."

Devon's frown deepened. "You're the owners now?"

"We are. We haven't talked about it much yet, but we're going to start calling contractors and see what they offer. We'll bring this house back to its old glory, and eventually, we'll move in."

Devon looked down. "When do you need me to leave?"

This was exactly what Yedley had expected. "We don't need you to leave."

Devon blinked up at them. "You don't?"

"No," Justin said. "Yedley and I talked, and we want you to stay here. We'd like you to help to renovate the house. We both realize you won't be able to work alongside the contractors, but we'll find you something to do, and we'll consider that rent. You can stay here indefinitely."

"I don't understand."

Yedley wasn't sure how to explain it better than Justin already had.

Justin cleared his throat. "You're a friend," he told Devon. "We might not have known each other long, but Yedley and I agree on this. We want you to feel safe, but we also want you to have a decent place to stay. This house isn't, but that's going to change. We don't want you to leave, and we thought that offering you a job would help keep you here."

They should have thought this through. The most important thing for Devon was that he stayed hidden, and someone was bound to find out if contractors started coming in and out of the house. But Justin was terrified that something would happen to Devon if he left, and he didn't want that to happen.

"Or we could find you another safe place," Yedley said.

Devon shook his head. "I'd like to stay here and help. But I'm not sure it's the wisest thing to do."

"It would be easier for us to help you if you told us what's going on," Justin pointed out. He hadn't pushed until now, but maybe now was the time to do it. He didn't want Devon to freak out and run away, but he couldn't continue living like this.

From how he behaved, he might intend to keep hiding indefinitely. That meant he didn't have contact with friends or family. He was alone, and since he was human, Justin suspected that sooner or later, the conditions he lived in would make him sick. It was a small miracle it hadn't yet, especially with the cold and the mold in the house.

"You can trust us," Yedley said. "I know these are just words, but we did our best to show that to you ever since we met. You're going to have to take a chance, and I hope you do. I hate the thought of you leaving and never seeing you again."

Devon shook his head. "Why?"

"Because we're friends. It doesn't matter that we don't know anything about your past. You let us in, and it was enough. I know I'm talking for both myself and Justin when I say we consider you family and that we want the best for you. And I'm sorry to say this, but at this point, I think that the best for you is to explain what's going on. We'll help you if you're hiding. We can make sure you're safe and that whoever you're running from doesn't find you. But we have to know who it is and what's going on. That way, it will be easier for us to do everything we can to keep you safe."

Justin fully expected Devon to say no, and possibly to leave, but instead, Devon leaned against the wall. The wall creaked, but it stayed up. "I never wanted to create problems for anyone," Devon said.

"You haven't," Yedley told him. "We're here because we want to be. We're offering you help because we want to help. But you need to allow us to."

"I'm running from my ex."

Justin wasn't surprised. It wasn't the first time he heard stories about abusive boyfriends, and it wouldn't be the last. "Why don't we sit down? You can tell us everything, and we can go from there."

Devon nodded and slid down the wall. He looked relieved, as if his legs couldn't quite hold him up. Whatever he was about to tell Justin and Yedley, it was obvious it was hard for him to deal with it.

"I met Elroy when I was nineteen. He didn't tell me I was his mate, but he heavily implied it, and I wanted to believe it. I don't have a family. I lived in foster homes, and I had to leave when I was eighteen. I've also never been very good at making friends, and when Elroy noticed me, I thought that was it. I thought I'd finally be able to have the family I've been yearning for forever since I was a kid. I think he maybe chose me because I was so alone in the world. He barely had to work to get in my life. I welcomed him and the dreams he brought with him until they became nightmares."

Yedley reached for one of the bottles of water lined against the wall. He cracked it open and offered it to Devon, who took it with a grateful smile. He took a few gulps before handing the bottle back to Yedley.

"In the beginning, everything was perfect. *Elroy* was perfect. Until he wasn't. He started getting jealous even though he had no reason to. He kept thinking I was cheating on him. That's when he started calling me dozens of times whenever I left the apartment. He didn't believe me when I told him I was at the grocery store or at work. I didn't know what to do, but I didn't want to lose him. That's why I agreed when he had demanded I quit my job. He told me he earned more than enough to support me, and I guess he did. But quitting my job was the worst thing I could have done. But I did it."

Justin wasn't surprised when Yedley took Devon's hand. Justin was approaching this more like an enforcer than a friend, but Yedley wasn't. He cared about Devon, and he wanted Devon to feel safe, even though he was remembering a terrible period of his life.

"Once I quit my job, Elroy locked me in the apartment. He didn't want me to leave. He took my phone away, and no matter how hard I tried, nothing I did was ever good enough for him. He always found a reason to yell at me, and eventually, to hurt me. But I still didn't leave."

"You didn't know where to go," Yedley said.

Justin had no idea how Devon felt. He'd always had his family, and later, the enforcers. Still, Devon's words hurt. Justin wanted to find this Elroy guy and hurt him like he'd hurt Devon. He hoped he'd have the opportunity to do just that.

"I didn't. I was terrified I'd end up on the streets, and I did. But in the beginning, I didn't realize that would be better than staying there, so I put up with him for much too long." Devon swallowed. "And I found out what Elroy is planning."

Justin frowned. "What is he planning?"

"He hates the council. That's why I decided to come to Gillham. I hoped it would be the last place where Elroy would look for me. I should have contacted the pack, but I was scared they wouldn't want to listen to me or that they'd contact Elroy."

"Kameron isn't like that. He would never force you to do anything, and he certainly wouldn't call your abuser to come to pick you up. I know you don't know him, but trust me on this."

"But I'm not a pack member."

"That doesn't mean he wouldn't be willing to help you. I'm new to this town, yet he's welcomed me. He and the pack are even paying for his house because they want Yedley and me to feel at home here. The same goes for you. I know how petrifying it has to be to reach out to someone you don't know like that, especially after what happened with Elroy, but at least think about it."

"What *is* Elroy planning?" Yedley asked.

Justin had almost already forgotten about that. He'd been focused on what Devon had been through and how afraid he was of reaching out to the pack.

"He hates the council," Devon repeated. "But for some reason, he hates the Gillham pack alpha even more. He created the Beasts. He's the one in command of the gang, and he's the reason the Beasts are in Gillham."

"They're not anymore," Justin pointed out.

"For now. But Elroy wants to destroy Gillham. He won't stop at anything to make that happen. That's what he's planning. He wants to take the Gillham pack alpha down, and the council along with him."

Shit. This wasn't what Justin had expected. He'd already suspected the *ex* bit and the fact that Devon's ex was abusive, but this was something else entirely. This was bigger than just an ex, and Justin wasn't sure how to make Devon realize that. He needed to, though, because the pack had to know what was coming for them — and who.

Yedley wanted to know more. Whoever this ever guy was, he was threatening Yedley's new life and his home. Yedley wouldn't let him do that, but how could he stop him?

"Justin is right. The pack rescued me from the Beasts, and they welcomed me even though I'm not comfortable with them yet. I don't know them, but I do know they won't hurt me. They have a solid reputation, and it's well-earned. They'll protect you if that's what you want, I promise." It might not be Yedley's place to make that kind of promise, but he believed it, and if the pack didn't step up, he would.

"But I don't have anything to give them. I know some things about Elroy, but no details on what he's planning to do. I just know he'll try to hurt the town and the pack as much as he can."

"And that's more than we knew until now," Justin intervened. "We had no idea who created the Beasts and who led the gang. Do you know why Elroy hates the pack and the council so much?"

Yedley hadn't known anything about the Beasts before he'd been taken. After he'd been released, Pryderi had explained they were shifters who believed humans were beneath them. They thought shifters should be the ones to rule the world, and they were working toward that goal. To obtain that, they created and sold drugs and were involved in human trafficking, including kidnapping people and selling them to the labs like Yedley had almost been. The Beasts might hate humans, but they didn't mind doing business with them.

"His brother. He never went into details because he didn't think it was my business, but something happened to his brother. He died or something, and Elroy thinks it was the pack's fault."

That probably wouldn't be useful to the pack, but Yedley didn't think Kam would care. Any bit of information could prove to be the detail they needed to eradicate the Beasts. They were gone from Gillham, but from what Devon was saying, it wouldn't be for long. Kam had been right to be careful and to send enforcers around to make sure there were no Beasts left in town. That wouldn't help if they came back, though.

"All right," Justin said. "Like I said, I understand why you're worried about talking to Kam. No matter how many promises I make, I realize it might not be enough for you to trust me and the pack. I won't insist for now because I don't think anything you just told me is vital for the pack's survival. Kam needs to know about this, if anything so he can start investigating into your ex, but I can let him know."

Devon shook his head, his eyes wide. "Please. I can leave if you want me to, but don't tell anyone I'm here. He'll find me. He has people everywhere, including in Gillham. They'll tell him I'm here, and he'll come for me."

Justin sighed. "I won't insist. I want to give you time to feel more comfortable. But I'd like it if you allowed me to at least tell Kameron you're here. Just in case something happens and your ex or anyone else connected to him finds out you're here. The pack will react faster if they're aware of your presence here. No one will force you to talk to Kameron, though. I promise."

The fear on Devon's face made Yedley's heart ache. He

wanted to help Devon, but how? He could try to keep Devon's body safe, but Devon had been abused and hurt. It would take more than a few weeks in a safe place to stay for him to feel comfortable and relax.

Justin rose from his crouch. "Why don't we start going around the house and make a list of what needs to be done? I know we can't start anything on our own, but I'm sure the contractors will be grateful we have an idea of what we want. Besides, I'd like them to start with one of the bedrooms and a bathroom. We can continue bringing food for you, Devon, but it will be better if you have a warm and clean place to sleep and a bathroom to shower and do everything else."

Devon scrambled to his feet. "You don't have to do that. I can continue living like this. I've been here for weeks, and it's more important for me to be safe than to be comfortable."

"You can be both. I don't want you to get ill, and that's bound to happen if you continue living this way. If you want to move out, that's fine, but otherwise, we'll make one of the bedrooms comfortable for you."

Devon held a hand out to Yedley, and Yedley gratefully took it. Hopefully, walking around the house would distract Devon for a while. Yedley knew how exhausting it was to always be afraid. Devon was hypervigilant, and Yedley wondered if he even slept at night. Probably not. He might take cat naps, but those weren't enough for him to fully rest. He might appear a bit better since the first time they'd met because he'd been eating regularly, but he still looked exhausted.

They filed out of the living room, and even though Yedley knew how bad the condition of the house was, he was still shocked. He hadn't explored it, limiting himself to visiting Devon in the living room. He was glad he hadn't, because he would have insisted that Devon move out the first day if he had seen what the entirety of the house looked like.

They paused in the entrance. The stairs facing the front door looked like they might come down if a mouse tried to climb them. The railing *had* come down, and it was lying at the bottom of the stairs, rotten wood and black metal twisting in eerie forms. Yedley peered upstairs, not willing to risk going there. He couldn't see much, though. There was a broken window on the first landing, but from his position, the upper floor looked like a gaping, dark hole.

He shivered and stepped back. The living room was to the left of the entrance, and he followed Devon and Justin to the right. He knew that was where the kitchen was, but he'd never entered it.

The walls were peeling just like in the rest of the house. Most of the cabinets had lost their doors, although a few were still hanging on. The floor was dirty, and while there was a kettle on the stove, Yedley wouldn't have touched it even if he'd been paid to do it.

"I know it looks bad right now," Justin started.

Yedley snorted. "Bad? That's an understatement."

Justin rolled his eyes. "But imagine how it could look once we renovate it. We'll get rid of everything, of course. Look at the space. Do you know how big this kitchen will be once we're done with it?"

Yedley didn't want to admit it, but he could imagine them living there. He'd never been much of a cook, but he'd been learning now that he lived with Nate, and he enjoyed it. What would it feel like to cook dinner for Justin? To welcome him when he came home from work? To have the house smell like cookies and bread? To have Pryderi, Nate, and Calvin over for dinner like a family?

The rest of the place was in pretty much the same shape. Everything would have to be torn down and rebuilt, and the amount of work it would take was petrifying. Yedley had no clue where to start, so it was good that Justin was planning to involve contractors. But Justin was excited, and it helped Yedley feel better about this.

He didn't regret buying the house with his mate. It would take time, but he was sure they could make it a home for them to live in and grow old together. And if it could be home for Devon too, Yedley was all for it. Family of blood didn't mean a lot to him except for his brother, but a family he and Justin would build with friends and people they cared for? That was everything Yedley had never allowed himself to dream of.

CHAPTER SEVEN

Justin kept an eye on Yedley, just in case, but he didn't seem to have trouble. He'd taken to the renovations easily, and Justin wondered if maybe he could make a job out of it. That was a conversation that could wait until later, though. Yedley was throwing himself entirely into the renovation, and it was good to see him this happy.

Devon was something else. He was helping, but only when the contractors weren't around. Justin had made sure they fixed a bedroom and its bathroom as well as they could, considering everything, and Devon hid out there when the contractors were working. Eventually, he would have to leave so the renovations could go on, but for now, this worked.

"You know, this would be faster and easier if you helped," Yedley said.

Justin looked at him to find him glaring with a hammer in his hand. He grinned. He could see Yedley wasn't angry at him. Besides, he was right. Justin was there to help, but instead, he was lost in his thoughts and staring at his mate.

No one would berate him for that, except maybe Yedley.

"I'm sorry. I got lost in my thoughts."

"I can see that. What were you thinking about?"

"Just that Devon won't be happy when he has to leave. And where will he go? I don't want him to feel like we're abandoning him, especially since we expect him to come back to live with us once the house is done, but I don't know how to tell him. The contractors have done a good job working around him until now, but you know that won't be possible

116

in the future."

Yedley frowned. "I think he already knows that."

"I'm sure he does, but knowing it and being suddenly faced with the reality isn't the same."

"We should talk to him, then."

They both turned toward the living room. That was always the room Devon tended to work in. Justin wasn't sure why, although he suspected it was because he felt safe there. It wasn't as dirty as it had been before, so that was a good thing, but he wished Devon would feel comfortable in the entire house. The three of them would live here, and Justin wanted the place to be home for Devon, not only a house. That would take time, and Justin and Yedley would do everything they could to help, but it was something Devon would have to work out on his own, mostly.

Justin nodded and reached for Yedley. Yedley didn't protest or move away, and Justin dragged him in his arms, kissing him.

A loud snort from behind them made both of them jump. Devon was there, grinning at them. "I thought the three of us were supposed to work today?" he said.

Justin laughed. "You caught us."

Devon looked happier. Justin wasn't sure how much of that was real and how much was a mask, but it was better than the terrified man he'd first met. They were working things out, and it was good for Devon.

A car door slammed outside, and Devon jumped. His eyes flew wide, and he looked at Justin on Yedley with what seemed to be a mix of fear and accusation. "You said the contractors wouldn't come around today."

"That's because they won't." It was Sunday, which was why the only ones working were the three of them.

Justin stepped away from Yedley and peered out the window. Part of his new team had come. They hadn't told him about it, and Justin was as surprised as Devon. "I didn't know about this, I promise." And Justin wasn't sure what to do with it. He knew Devon was terrified, and he didn't want him to suffer, but maybe this wasn't a bad thing. "They're my friends. They won't hurt you, and if you ask them not to, they won't tell anyone you're here." Even though Devon would eventually have to meet Kameron, he wasn't comfortable with it right now, and that was okay.

Devon looked around, obviously searching for a way to escape. Justin wanted to reassure him, but how should he do that? "Why don't you stay here? I'll go out there and ask what's going on, okay?"

Yedley moved toward Devon, taking his hand and murmuring something to him. Justin left both of them there and went to meet his team members. They didn't know about Devon, and Justin didn't think any of them had seen him well enough the day they'd explored this house to recognize him, especially now that Devon was cleaner and was regularly eating. Still, he didn't want them to wonder or to ask questions.

"What are you doing here? I didn't expect you guys."

Davis grinned and thrust a six-pack of beer into Justin's hands. "That's because we didn't plan this. We started talking about where you were and why, and we decided we might as well use our free day to help you."

"You do realize I've hired contractors, right? They're the ones doing the bulk of the job."

"Yet you and your mate are here working today. Come on. I promise we won't break anything that doesn't need to be broken."

Justin didn't want to say no to Davis' offer. He wanted to become closer to his new team, to spend time with them, to get to know them. Being on the job wasn't the best way to make that happen, and this was a chance for Justin to become friends with them. "Just let me check one thing, and I'll be right back." Justin would allow them in only if Devon was okay with it.

He was relieved to find Devon was still with Yedley when he went back in. He cleared his throat, getting both men's attention. "It's my team members. Like I said, I didn't expect them to come. It's a surprise for me, but I can tell them to leave if that's what you want, Devon."

"Maybe you should let them in," Yedley said. Devon jerked away from him, but Yedley held onto his hand. "I know you don't trust anyone but Justin and me. I won't push you, but you can't continue hiding in here. You'll eventually have to talk to Kameron, and it would be good for you to meet people. Justin and I can vouch for his teammates. They're good people. They wouldn't be enforcers otherwise because the council is very picky when it comes to the people they hire. Don't tell them who you are or why you here if you don't want to, but give them a chance, please."

Devon was pale, but to Justin's surprise, he didn't run to the stairs. "What should I tell them, then?"

"I'll say you're my cousin," Justin said.

Devon blinked. "We don't look alike."

"We don't have to."

"You're a werewolf. I'm a human."

"Not everyone with shifter genes can shift. Besides, I doubt you'll allow any of them to go close enough to you to smell you. It'll be fine. We can tell them you're my cousin, and if you feel overwhelmed, say you have a headache and go to your room. They'll understand."

Justin didn't expect Devon to say yes, but Devon slowly nodded. "They'll stay away from me if I don't want them close?"

"You just have to say the word. I promise."

"Okay, then. As long as you tell them not to come too close to me, I'm okay with it. I trust you and Yedley. I know you'll protect me if I need to be."

That was huge for Devon. Justin knew he was more comfortable with them, but not this much. They were probably the only people he trusted in the world, and Justin felt humbled by that. He didn't know what would happen with Devon and with his ex, with the Beasts and the pack, but Devon was part of his family now, just like Yedley. He'd do everything he had to do to keep them safe and protect them.

YOU MAY ALSO ENJOY THE FOLLOWING FROM EXTASY BOOKS INC:

Christmas Swan
Catherine Lievens

Excerpt

Curtis had no idea where he was.

He'd opened his eyes a few seconds later, and he didn't recognize the bedroom — or the bed — he was in. Initially, he'd thought he'd had a one-night stand and that he was still in the guy's bed. It wasn't something he'd normally do, but his life had been anything but normal in the past couple of weeks, so who knew. But then he'd tried to sit up, and both his arm and his head hurt. The sharp pain in his forehead had been enough to clear his thoughts, but while he remembered the fox that had attacked him and that he'd managed to fly away, he still had no idea how he'd ended up in a comfortable, warm bed instead of in the freezing snow.

He raised the blanket that covered him. He was still naked, and he could too easily imagine how he'd ended up here. Had it been a sweet old lady? Or maybe a family with kids? Curtis didn't want to stick around to find out, even though he knew he owed whoever had found him his life. He could come back later, once he was covered and able to look them in the eyes.

He pushed himself up using the arm that wasn't wounded and peered at the other one. The fox had bit his wing, and he had no idea how bad the wound was. He'd have to take off the bandages that now covered it once he was home. His head still hurt, too, but it was nothing a good painkiller wouldn't help with.

He swung his feet off the bed, and the door opened.

Curtis grabbed the blanket and made sure his groin was covered, but there was little he could do for his legs and his upper body. A man came in carrying a tray and humming to himself, but he squeaked when he saw Curtis was awake, and he almost dropped the tray.

"What do you think you're doing?" the man asked.

"Getting up."

The man put the tray on the dresser. "I can see that, but you're wounded." He looked at Curtis' arm, but his gaze kept moving to Curtis' chest, and his cheeks were flushed with pink. He cleared his throat. "You should get back to bed. I'll find you some clothes now that you're awake."

Curtis didn't have much of a choice. He slid back into bed and made sure everything that needed to be covered was covered. "Thank you. I'm Curtis."

The man smiled. "I'm Manuel. Wait here. You'll be more comfortable once you're dressed."

Curtis agreed with that. He watched as Manuel disappeared through a door and reappeared with what looked like a t-shirt and a pair of sweats. He held them out. "These are the biggest I have. I'm smaller than you, so they might be tight, but I can't do much more."

"I'm sure they're fine." Curtis took them and started to get up, but he remembered he was still naked. His arm hurt, but with Manuel's help, he managed to get the t-shirt on. The sweats were a bit trickier without leaving the bed, but Manuel blushed and turned around so Curtis could have privacy.

Curtis' headache was still firmly there, so he flopped back again the pillows and groaned. Manuel turned around, frowning. "Are you okay?"

"Headache."

"I'll grab you some painkillers." He went through another door—Curtis suspected that was the bathroom—and came back with a bottle. He grabbed a glass of water from the tray he'd brought in and sat on the edge of the mattress, handing Curtis the glass and the bottle. He was so close that Curtis could smell him, and Curtis' heart suddenly tried to get out of his chest as it raced in surprise and shock.

This wasn't how Curtis had thought the day would go. He hadn't expected to be attacked by a fox, and he certainly hadn't expected to meet his mate.

"So, how did it happen?" Manuel asked, jerking Curtis out of his shock.

"What?" he managed to croak, but that was all his brain could manage.

"Well, I found you naked face down in the snow. You should have a good story about it, and I can't wait to hear it."

Damn it. Curtis couldn't tell Manuel how he'd ended up freezing his balls off. That would mean telling him he was a swan shifter, and possibly, that they were mates, and Curtis was not ready for Manuel to throw him out.

He licked his lips. "I'll be honest. I'm not sure. I think I hit my head because I can't remember much, and it hurts like a bitch."

"Oh!" Manuel grabbed the bottle of painkillers from Curtis' hand and opened it. "Take this. You'll feel better."

Curtis obeyed. His swan was pleased with the way their mate was taking care of them, which was better than having it squawking in his mind because they'd been attacked by a fox, but it wasn't helping. Curtis had no idea what to do with, well, everything. He didn't know how to deal with meeting his mate, and with the fact that Manuel had already seen him naked and that he didn't remember it.

"I should go home," he murmured.

"Nope. You should stay here for a bit and let me call

someone who can come pick you up. Unless I can drive you somewhere? I don't like to drive in the snow, especially not at night, but I can make an exception."

"I'll call one of my brothers." Curtis groaned. They were going to make fun of him forever. "They're going to have a field trip with this."

"Well, you can't deny it is kind of funny, at least now that you're warm and safe." Manuel frowned. "Unless you were hurt. Maybe I should take you to the hospital."

"I'm fine. I might not remember, but I'm sure no one hurt me."

"If you say so." Manuel didn't look convinced, but Curtis couldn't tell him the truth, not yet.

ABOUT THE AUTHOR

Catherine lives in Italy, country of good food and hot men. She used to write fantasy as a child, but it was reading her first gay erotic romance novel that made her realize that that was what she really wanted to write.

After graduating from college in English language and translation, she divides her day between writing, reading, taking care of her son and reading some more.

You can find her on Facebook and Twitter or on her website: authorcatherinelievens.wordpress.com

Email: lievens.catherine@gmail.com

Newsletter: http://eepurl.com/c-uvKn

Bookbub: https://www.bookbub.com/authors/catherine-lievens

www.ingramcontent.com/pod-product-compliance
Lightning Source LLC
Chambersburg PA
CBHW060633130626
46555CB00002B/778